CLAN ZHAKKARI

JASON TEJIRI BOJE

CLAN ZHAKKARI

Second Edition: January 2026

Self-Published by: Jason Boje

Cover Design by: Jason Boje

Interior Layout by: Jason Boje

CONTENTS

Dedicated to Melodia Kemmer Okoro.
God rest her soul.

A FERVID CHILDHOOD

CIVCAZ, as an ancient land, was unorthodox compared to the lands surrounding it at the time.

The seasons alternated solely between scorching desert heat and the cold of flooding rains. Instead of a traditional monarch found in most other nations, a tiered system of warrior-scholar clans was in place, where families ruled together over different parts of their nation. In place of the many gods that were mythologised at the time, the people chose to worship the very essences of human vitality, ingenuity, regality, and justice.

Large, robust, and of an aggressive yet anxious constitution, Kingsley Zhakkari was restless. His body shook as he stood amongst a rank of Civcaz warriors. In his youth, such anxiety would have eaten at his soul. But years of experience into middle age saw him able to utilise this fear, fuelling his preparations for battle.

Like the hundreds of men who joined him within the confines of a great cave lit up by purple flames, Kingsley wore traditional Civcaz armour. A sturdy breastplate of gold, welded-together linen layered thick and trousers made from the same material, fastening the two pieces together with a black scabbard belt holding a sword on one side and another weapon of choice on the other. Kingsley had chosen the two-pronged shortsword, a common blade of choice for Commonsclan Zhakkari. All the men who made up that particular warrior faction were primed for a fight, only having one more act to carry out before descending into bloodshed. The worship ritual.

Every man in this army turned to face the westernmost crevice of the cave. Each of them reached underneath their breastplate to retrieve a scroll, which they laid on the back of the man in front of them, or on a wall. They muttered under their breath as they read the scroll as fast as humanly possible. As soon as a warrior finished reading his scroll, he would use it to wipe down any dirt or marks present on his armour. Once done, they tucked the scroll away and turned until each of them was face to face with their fellow man. Each warrior struck the man they saw with a blow across the face and allowed the same to be done to them. They bowed, showing respect to their fellow warrior, and completing the ritual.

It was not known whether such a ritual had real magical properties or any genuine effects on one's soul, for that matter. Though if you asked any of these men, they would assure you it did. Having completed the ritual this time, as with every other time, Kingsley felt a surge of vital energy pumping through his body in place of his blood. As if a god had taken refuge within his very soul.

The legions of men exited the cave immediately, marching out onto the grasslands in which their fighting would take place. The enemy met them in open combat, a legion of men wearing very similar garb and charging at them across the battlefield of dead yellow grass.

Both factions showed little care for restraint, willing to meet the full force of an opponent's blade. There were no considerations for personal safety in each warrior's mind, only vital impulse.

As Kingsley engaged his first man in one-on-one combat, he felt the very virtues he had just worshipped with his fellow man in the purple-flamed cave surging him forward in every movement. His adherence to regality allowed him to dodge every swing of his opponent's blade with grace and beauty. His adherence to ingenuity allowed him to quickly identify his opponent's weak spot - a delayed pivot of his left leg when swinging his blade. His adherence to vitality allowed him the boldness to decide against dodging a strike of the blade, letting it clash against his armour as he used the opportunity to knock his enemy down with a push-kick. Finally, his adherence to justice saw him give the man a simple and clean death. He sliced across his neck in one seamless motion, using the momentum to immediately engage another opponent adjacent to him.

By Civcaz standards, Kingsley Zhakkari was a mediocre warrior. But through belief in the spiritual essence of the ritual and the virtues that came with it, he fought as if he were the bravest conqueror.

***

Kingsley Zhakkari woke up, having felt like he had been put to sleep for days on end. With a mouth filled with blood and a head dazed, he was astonished by how he could still feel the air in his lungs. What he last remembered was being bested by an opponent in battle who clubbed him over the head with a blunt weapon, then lunged to finish him with his blade. But as he woke up on that battlefield, he found the very same man draped over him with a double-slit gash deep in his gut.

3

Kingsley saw his two-pronged blade discarded on the floor, inches away from his open palm. He put two and two together. Once again, his instincts had only just about saved him. Though he was grateful for having saved himself from certain death in another battle, he felt no triumph. He was paralysed with fear. He felt he was living on borrowed time.

"Rise," a comrade from the cave said as he approached, offering him a hand. "What kind of warrior lies on his back after an emphatic victory?"

As his comrade helped pull his rise, Kingsley's eyes scoured the battlefield. Never a gorier mess had he seen in his life. He had grown used to seeing dead men scattered across blood-soaked fields over the years. Yet the massacre on display that day was still enough to turn his stomach. He lost count of the number of gouged eyes, severed limbs, and ripped-out throats he saw as they walked to meet with the rest of their surviving faction. One of the corpses seemed to catch his eye, an enemy corpse. Though the face was torn to mangled shreds as if attacked by a wild beast, Kingsley recognised the unfortunate lost soul.

"Emmanuel," he whispered, stopping to observe.

"You knew this man?" his comrade asked him.

"We trained in the same warrior group as children and fought many battles together as young adults. I never would've thought I'd be looking over his dead body on a battlefield," Kingsley sighed. He shook his head in grief. His comrade laughed.

"That's what happens to you when you're on the wrong side of history," he scoffed, kicking the dead body in its side. "Thank the virtues we're not."

The man burst into a fit of raucous laughter, nudging Kingsley in the side in a playful manner. Kingsley smiled back weakly. That comment did not give him the sense of security it ought to have.

***

Kingsley returned to his home in much lower spirits despite their victory. The passion for battle that fuelled his previously high spirits diminished after its conclusion and was replaced by the subtler mixture of anxiety and aggression he was known to carry. Although he loved seeing his family, they were the root cause of the fears he had about the world. Especially concerning the battle he had just witnessed.

Kingsley arrived at the front of his Hustan, an abode granted to any family that was the leader of a clan on a plot of land, regardless of their station. Whether they be a mighty Kingsclan, an influential Arisclan, or a simple Commonsclan like the Zhakkari family. Most Hustans shared a similar appearance. A simple truncated block of fine brick standing hundreds of feet tall. Including Clan Zhakkari's. Outside the large door of golden-bordered wood were four common warriors with their weapons at the ready, defenders of their land. The defenders parted ways as they allowed the clan leader into his home.

***

Upon entering the Hustan, Kingsley increased the pace at which he marched, desperate to spend as little time through the halls as possible. He headed to the last of a series of black wooden doors at the end of the building.

The door led him to a 'room' which would have been an open field behind the Hustan had it not been for the roof built over it. An indoor yard of vibrant flora with trees, flowers, and stone, all manufactured and refined beyond their natural state to serve different purposes, whether it be for climbing, for sword-fighting, or for running over.

5

Kingsley created this indoor yard to be a place of contained training and development. The stress he carried with him into the room dissipated as he took note of his wife at the front of the room. She watched over his four children using the yard for its purposes. His beautiful family were doing their duties.

"Good afternoon, dearie," Kingsley's wife, Faith, greeted when she noted his presence. She was a tall and slender woman with a contrastingly soft and round face.

Faith gave him a smile that would have filled him with adoration and warmth had it not been for her body language. The sleeves of her traditional multi-coloured Clan Zhakkari tribal dress were creased from a tight crossing of her arms. Like him, she was tense and anxious.

"If it is such a good afternoon, then why are you so tense?" he asked her.

Faith sighed. "I always tell myself you'll be fine after every battle, and you always are. But my body can't help but shiver as if otherwise."

"I can't help but shiver as if otherwise, either. Especially in the middle of battle," Kingsley said. "But I persevere, for I know the virtues are with me."

Kingsley comforted her with an arm around her waist. She looked up at him, smiling, appreciating the warmth of the gesture as she uncrossed her arms.

"And now you should tell me why *you're* tense," she said, turning the questions on him.

Kingsley's smile faded as he bit the inside of his mouth.

"I didn't tell you beforehand, but the battle we fought today wasn't against a foreign faction. It was against Clan Godwin," Kingsley revealed. "I'm still not sure whether the land's turn against them was just."

Faith nodded, jittering as she quickly assessed the dilemma in her head. She crossed her arms once more.

"Whilst we can commend Clan Godwin for having founded and allowed for our land to prosper, we must admit they grew into an arrogant, superior, and oppressive force," Faith assessed. "It may be unsavoury, but fighting against them *is* just. Right?"

"That's right," he agreed with her, sounding resolute yet appearing unsure. Faith found his manner of reply to be peculiar but sought not to unravel.

"Our darling children," Kingsley said, breaking the silence after a few minutes. He motioned towards the yard in front of them. "Are they doing well with their schooling?"

"More or less," Faith said.

The couple looked to their first child, Ezekiel, as he trained on the field. With a longsword fit for a grown man, he hacked away at a stone structure on the corner, gritting his teeth until he could taste blood. Ezekiel was twelve at the time, yet had the size, strength, and aggression of a man already of age. He grunted and growled with the fury of a beast, attacking the stone with such force that one would think it had insulted his family line.

"Ezekiel," Kingsley said. "The boy was born with enough pugnacity for ten warriors."

Faith laughed. "Remember when you used to try to beat it out of him?"

"Unfortunately," Kingsley sighed with shame.

Efforts to use physical discipline on the young man growing up proved fruitless, as the boy would just fight back. The more Ezekiel fought, the more force Kingsley had to use, until one day, he was inches away from killing him.

Kingsley rubbed his hands as if they were still stained with the blood from the savage beating he gave his son that day.

"Grace's skills are improving," Faith commented, turning her attention towards their second child.

A dignified young woman, ten years of age, Grace held her bow and arrow as if marksmanship was second nature to her. Standing on a concrete shore on one side of the yard's pond, she squinted one eye and aimed for a splatter of red blood on the wall at the other side. Grace reached into the quiver slung across her back, grabbing three arrows. She placed all three in the bow and shot them at the target. None missed. Grace turned her nose up in a haughty manner, smirking to herself in satisfaction. With her eyes closed, she skipped around the pond humming her praises in smug glee, basking in her glory as if an audience was watching her.

"Yes, but her arrogance is unbecoming of a young lady," Kingsley observed. Faith nodded in agreement as she watched her daughter dance and boast to herself.

They looked to their fourth and youngest child. A small and sweet girl of only seven years old with her mother's soft, darling features and father's fretful eyes.

Promise engaged in no such training as Ezekiel and Grace. She calmly walked a thin barrier at the end of the yard, watering each of the blooming golden flowers with the careful tip of a chalice.

"Are you sure you don't want her to take part in the same physical schooling as Grace and the boys?" Faith asked.

Kingsley shook his head. "She doesn't have the constitution for it," he dismissed. Faith conceded with a nod of her head backwards.

"Our precious Promise," she whispered.

Kingsley's eyes scanned the fields once more. He could not find his third child.

"Where's Samuel?" he asked, eyebrows furrowed and voice laced with building vexation.

Faith pointed upwards, bringing his attention to a tree in the westernmost corner of the yard. Kingsley found that his son, Samuel, nine years of age, was no longer engaged in the training assigned to him.

The young boy hung upside down, lying on a sturdy tree branch as he read a scroll. Samuel had an eccentric smile plastered on his face, a smile that Kingsley could not tell whether it was due to how amusing what he was reading was or how quickly the blood was rushing to his head from his upside-down hanging. Either way, it irritated him.

"Once again, he's ignoring his assigned schooling to do nonsense," Kingsley spat.

"Perhaps it isn't a part of his constitution either," Faith suggested.

Kingsley shook his head. "We can't afford for that to be the case! You know this!"

Faith stared at her cheerfully eccentric son, not responding. Kingsley kept staring at him, too, a controlled anger subtly bubbling beneath the surface.

Samuel was a smart boy. He could respect that. When it came to their scholarly duties, Samuel was the child who remained the most focused and dedicated. What he could not respect was the flouting of his duties as a budding warrior. Kingsley thought back to when his son was much younger. The boy had been so sickly growing up that it stunted his development, making him much smaller than a typical Zhakkari male in both height and weight. Kingsley attributed the sickness and the stunting it caused to why Samuel did not take his physical schooling duties seriously.

9

Kingsley rubbed his head. The stress that had melted away was building within him again. A tension headache in the pit of the skull caused him to wince in pain, a face his wife recognised all too well.

"We need to stop worrying about whether they will be fit to face what the future will bring," Faith emphasised. "We have to trust that they'll be fine."

"Will they?! Do you believe that?!" Kingsley asked.
Faith was slow to give him an answer, clearly suggesting she felt otherwise.

"Well, if not, we're doomed," she finally said. "For the sake of this land, let's assume they will be."

A KINGLY MEETING

SAMUEL Zhakkari had recently aged a year past being two decades old. Yet he retained his youthful eccentricity, as if he were still that nine-year-old reading a scroll upside down on the training yard tree.

That morning, he had found himself underneath a tree instead. He woke, his nose assaulted by pollen as he realised that he had accidentally fallen asleep outside once again.

A series of scrolls containing different forms of information lay scattered on his lap. Some were legendary tales of old, some were accounts of battles long gone, and some were lists of policies implemented by different clans that made it into official Civcaz law.

In his half-baked state of waking from sleep, Samuel was unsure as to why he came out there to read with his scrolls or what he was planning to do before he fell to slumber. He stood to his feet and saw a cliff only a few short paces away from his spot. Being one to sleepwalk, he realised he could have launched himself to his death.

Samuel walked to the edge of the cliff and, upon arrival, remembered his reason for coming here. To propel the inspiration that he would need to pursue his future goals.

Samuel marvelled at the sights beyond the cliff. From this vantage point, he could see all the land that belonged to his family and more. Below him was a lake that acted as an oasis in the warm climate of North-West Civcaz. Beyond the oasis and across the shores were a series of hills where the sand turned to hard, rough grass.

Upon these hills of grass, he saw a collection of farmlands and stone houses structured across the land to make a large, uniform village, vast yet dull. The only thing close to a sight of beauty was the Clan Zhakkari Hustan, but even that was surrounded by dry farmland. It seemed like the oasis had stolen all the moisture and left him and his people with the drabbest of greenery in its wake. Samuel smiled mischievously, tutting as if to scold the land itself for the crime of being too dreary.

"If only I could use those beautiful oasis waters to wash away the grime that is the hills of our civilisation," he said to himself. "No. Knowing our luck, it'd flood the crops rather than water them. Our farmlands are bad enough."

Samuel chuckled softly, overly amused at his quips as he often found himself to be.

Though he could not wash the land clean and make it grow physically, he planned to do so in essence. In the years it took him to come of age, there was only one thing Samuel was convinced was a fact. That the only person capable of bettering Clan Zhakkari was him.

***

"No way did you fucking win again!" complained the tavern-keeper. He threw his metal cards on the table in anger. With a sliding finger on top, Samuel collected all the metal cards for himself, a giddy smile on his face.

He opted to spend his morning in one of the dull buildings on the *hills of civilisation* he had looked over earlier, a simple establishment with black polished rocks for the patrons to sit on. Only this morning, most were empty as these patrons had left their tables and gathered to watch Samuel play the tavern keeper in a game of Blade Cards.

"How'd you guess it right every time?" the drink seller asked. Samuel laughed.

In the game, each player received a series of identical metal cards. Most were made of dull metal, and a select few were sharp enough to be used as a blade.

Players traded cards, where the goal of the game was for you to deceive the other player into picking the bladed cards and for you to avoid them when it was your turn, using your intuition. The knicks and cuts on the tavern keeper's fingers contrasted with Samuel's pristine scarless fingers, showing who was winning.

"I really am too good," Samuel gloated.

"More like too clever for your own good," scoffed one of the tavern regulars who surrounded the table to watch the match. "When are you going to use that brain of yours for our benefit instead of just embarrassing us all the time?"

The other men murmured, equally impressed with and irritated by Samuel. A reaction he was used to.

"Aye, give the boy some credit. He's the one who drew up those plans for the canals in my fields!" interjected a portly man, coming to Samuel's defence. "Without his help, my land would have gone to shit!"

"And mine," added another tavern member. Samuel shrugged with humility.

"Also, I'm letting you all keep the betting money you lost today. *That's* a benefit," Samuel said to the tavern regular who called him out.

The man groaned in response to the third-born Zhakkari's giddy laughs. If one were lucky, they could easily win a couple of rounds of the carded blade game. If one were both lucky *and* clever, one could win most rounds. Samuel won every single round that day.

"Here, just take it," the tavern keeper said, dashing a fistful of coins over the table, some still stained with the dried blood of his losses. "A bet's a bet."

"No. I already said I'm letting you all keep your money. Spend it on someone who deserves it, like your wife or children," Samuel said.

The tavern-keeper smiled, coarse yet appreciative. "Bad enough he has to be a cocky fuck when he wins. He insists on acting all altruistic about it as well."

He stood to leave as Samuel shooed him away with a nod and smile. The man laughed to himself as he returned to his station behind the rocky slab of a bar. Some of the patrons who had gathered dispersed to order more drinks, whilst others closed in on Samuel's table.

"Watch, I'll be the first person here to beat this little shit," the man who had called him out earlier said as he took up the tavern-keeper's seat across from Samuel.

"It'll have to be a quick round. I have somewhere to be soon," Samuel told the man.

"Where the fuck do you need to be?" the man asked. Samuel's eyes fixated on the man intensely before answering. "Remember when you said I should use my brain to benefit this land more?" Samuel asked. The man nodded in confirmation. "Well, where I'm going, I'll finally be able to do that on a *much grander* scale."

The smile Samuel flashed at the men around the table did not resemble that of the future saviour of their land. It would have better suited the face of a devil.

***

No longer on Clan Zhakkari land, Samuel travelled to the centre of the main Civcaz area, the portion of the land in which most of the nation's most famous and infamous Arisclans and Kingsclans lived. He was yet to earn the privilege of visiting the Hustans of one of these great families, though he was as close as a person of his station could be. Few Commonsclan members, clan leaders or otherwise, could say they had spent time in the stratagem-quarters of a Kingsclan.

Samuel was in a room filled with gold trinkets won in battle and carefully arranged on either side of a carved-out court floor. The ceiling was high enough to throw a spear upwards and not have to worry about it landing for a while.

He sat at a table across from a very different type of person than his company at the tavern. Though close in age to Samuel, he carried himself like a man much older. The man's hair had started to subtly grey, as if to match his demeanour. He wore the sturdy breastplate of gold, welded-together linen layered thick that most Civcaz warriors and even scholars wore, with a grey Hustan logo on the front. The symbol of Clan Khoza. A part of Samuel could not believe he had managed to secure a meeting with William, the head of Kingsclan Khoza.

"Your records look good, I must admit," William said with a stiff upper lip. He had been perusing through a series of scrolls Samuel had placed on his desk. "I've heard of the good work you've done for your clan, but I didn't realise you were this much of a scholar."

"You should."

"And why's that?"

"We did some schooling together as children."

William paused his reading. He squinted his eyes as he studied Samuel's face.

"Oh, yes, that's right, my apologies," he said. "How could I have forgotten?"

"It's alright. We didn't talk back then. I'm surprised you remembered so quickly."

"You were the small child at the back of the room who'd refuse to work with the others, weren't you?"

"I was."

"I don't blame you, considering the way the other children treated you back then," William said. "Some of the other children seemed hell-bent on tormenting you."

"They were," Samuel answered rather bitterly, recalling a time they had set fire to his tunic as a joke. A horrific scar on the small of his back made sure he could never forget.

"What are the odds we meet again, especially with how much has changed over the years? My family have risen to the rank of Kingsclan, and now you are looking to earn a seat on the Shared Council," William said. "That is what you're here for, correct?"

"Correct," Samuel said, his smile widening.

William looked over Samuel carefully as he put his scrolls and documents to the side.

"Your family, Clan Zhakkari, is one of the most influential Commonsclans that Civcaz has to offer," William stated. "You have more land to your names than some Arisclans."

"Yes, but most of that is either dry or land that takes a considerable amount of effort to keep from dying. Not exactly royal soil," Samuel chuckled.

"Is that why you want a seat on the council? To gain more royal soil?" William asked, accusatory. "Are you looking to move your family up to the rank of an Arisclan? Or perhaps even a Kingsclan?"

"If that ends up being the case, it will only be a bonus," Samuel said, shrugging. "What I want is to implement policies that will help the people of this land."

William's face tightened in curiosity. "What kind of policies?"

Samuel rubbed his hands together like he was preparing for a meal, excited to tell all.

"My father, Kingsley Zhakkari, used to have us perform a series of trials that our mother would watch over in our youth, both physical and mental," he explained. "Though I hated them, I believe those trials are what made my siblings and I so skilled. I believe the same results can be achieved with the children of today."

Samuel did not speak to his siblings often anymore, nor did he want to. But he had to respect their competencies.

"You believe the same should be done for children today? Why is that?" William asked.

"Children these days don't seem to worship the virtues as much as we were taught growing up. I'm not suggesting that we *have* to make them worship the virtues, but we can create systems that will help them develop their vitality, ingenuity, regality, and justness. Systems similar to my father's," Samuel explained. "An updated, revolutionised version of my father's methods could work to secure a brighter future for the Land of Civcaz as a whole."

Samuel waited as William mulled over what he proposed. The Clan Khoza member released a deep, thoughtful sigh.

"Interesting," William said, leaning back into his chair with a smile. "I'll take all you've said into account when considering you for the role."

Samuel liked the sound of that. He smirked.

***

Samuel walked through the mainland with smug satisfaction later in the day. He could already see himself sitting on the Kingsclan council. He would secure the role. He knew it.

It had been a while since he travelled through the mainland, the heart of all opportunity in the Civcaz, the place where the grandest clans held land. Its essence beguiled him, but its current presentation left much to be desired. He could not tell if his expectations were set too high or if the land had worsened since his last visit.

The infrastructure still impressed. The Hustans owned by the Arisclans and Kingsclans were made of finer stone of the golden-onyx variety, making the Zhakkari's Hustan seem like a mud hut in comparison. The streets were constructed with well-tempered stone cut to perfection and smoothed out. The estate homes of the people on said streets were taller and livelier, and there was much more traffic through the area than Samuel was used to. He could see why. The marketplaces on offer were of a much higher quality than those of his land. They had fresher fruit, heartier meat, and kinder barterers at these large stands. All those qualities were still to the standard that he expected. It was the behaviour of the people that disappointed him.

Samuel arrived at an area on the fringe of the town he found himself in. Many people congregated at a hexagonal stone platform where a spectacle was being carried out.

Tens of thousands of people joined in chants as they urged a dozen men to engage in the most unholy of acts.

A frail man on the brink of starvation was held up against a giant slab of rock. A sword had been driven through the top of his scalp, nailing him to the slab as blood poured from his head and screams flooded out of his mouth. Six men flayed the man using whips encrusted with diamond blades. His dark skin had been brutalised until it was fresh pink. Whilst this was done, six other men held out the man's feet, driving small blades as sharp as a shark's tooth underneath each toenail over and over. There could not have been a man in all the lands experiencing as much pain as he was at that moment.

The sickness the sight caused Samuel was gradually being overridden by fascination as he wondered how the man was still alive. The unlucky man's screams harboured enough agony to shake the core of even the strongest of warriors. Yet the onlookers were celebratory of his fate rather than sympathetic. Samuel pushed forward into the crowd to get a better look at the man, and he realised why. It was the third son of the most infamous Kingsclan.

"John Godwin," he muttered to himself in realisation. Samuel remembered how his father used to come home from battles where warriors from many clans would band together to attack Clan Godwin. He remembered his mother saying something about how they were once a good clan responsible for founding their land, but became too haughty and violent and thus needed to be dealt with. Over the years, the Godwins went from the most powerful clan to the land's literal whipping boys. Personally, Samuel had no real issue with their particular Kingsclan. The only ill will that he felt towards them growing up was envy. He coveted their high status at the top of the Civcaz hierarchy back then. He did not envy their position in society nowadays.

Samuel could not stand to watch this crude execution anymore, leaving before he could see John Godwin die.

"Any appetite I might have developed this afternoon has well and truly been destroyed," Samuel quipped to himself as he marched away. He could not believe what he saw. Public torture? In the mainland of all places? He would not have believed it had he not seen it himself. Such a spectacle did not belong at the heart of their civilisation, the birthplace of the virtues they worshipped.

He decided that once he had his seat on the council and collected enough power, he would demand that such vulgarities never take place. Especially not on the mainland.

A SIBLING REUNION

GRACE Zhakkari stood by the window of a Hustan, hands placed on her sides as she gazed at the beauty of the rising morning sun. She stared upon it with such gratitude that you would think the sun had only risen for her sake alone.

As if to further validate the overabundance of pride she already possessed, a group of people could be seen looking up in awe from outside the Hustan. Teenage boys about half a decade younger than she was assembled to bear witness to her beauty. Usually, Grace would let them stare, pretending to be unaware of their presence. That day, however, she decided to slowly fix her sight on them and smile. Nervous at what they perceived as their first instance of being caught, the boys stopped their staring and disassembled, some awkwardly walking or even running away.

Grace chuckled as they scampered off.

***

Grace sported the black and red colours of a traditional cotton-blend Clan Zhakkari dress that perfectly fit her well-formed figure. Whilst a young woman proudly wearing such garms would usually be found waltzing through her clan's Hustan, Grace waltzed through common rooms much grander. She pushed open an impressive set of double doors that felt of wood but were flawlessly painted to give the impression of being made of gold. Above this door was an emblem made from true gold. A depiction of a beautiful, delicate lioness. The emblem of Clan Bello.

Grace entered the dining room with a pompous flair. She swanned around an immense table before taking her seat. As hearty a meal as could be asked for waited for her on the table. The sweetest bread, the highest quality eggs, the finest cuts of meat, and a smooth sugary drink to lift her already high spirits. Her plate was a sight for sore eyes, as was her company around the table. She was sitting among the family that made up Arisclan Bello:

Simon Bello, a square-jawed father of hardened, handsome features yet irreverent eyes. Helene Bello, an elegant mother carrying the vibrant beauty and extravagant jewellery of a woman much younger. Michel Bello, the son who was a couple of years older than Grace, with the delicate good looks of a fairy tale hero that mismatched his perpetually stern expression. Finally, Jacqueline Bello, the soft but sour-faced young girl whom Grace had been acquainted with since childhood.

Grace fit in as if this were her family. Some would say that she fit in more with Bellos than her Zhakkari bredrin.

"Have we decided the main event for the dry season gala yet?" Michel asked as they ate. He made a point to clear his throat and crack his knuckles before he spoke, making it known that they had been neglecting the topic too much for his liking.

"Must we host *another* gala? Is it by force?" his father scoffed with derision.

"We promised the people of our land a celebration for the dry season, so they're expecting one. Who are we to deny them?" Helene asked, flamboyantly waving her hands.

"To go back on our promise would be unbecoming," Michel added in agreement with his mother.

Simon rolled his eyes, accepting their arguments. "What do you have in mind?"

Michel's eyes locked with Grace's as he took a sip of his drink. "Perhaps you could sing," he suggested.

"Perhaps I could," Grace agreed with a smirk. Michel smirked back at her as the two shared a brief yearning gaze. A gaze that was a little too long for his sister's liking.

Jacqueline twisted in her seat a touch. "Stop badgering Grace for performances! We can't rely on her for every event of ours!" she complained.

"No, it's fine, Jacq, I like performing," Grace said. A major understatement on her part. She adored it.

"Why don't we give your voice a rest this time, Gracey?" Jacqueline suggested, resting a soft hand on her shoulder. Grace ignored her, her eyes still on Michel.

"Then what should the main event be?" Michel asked.

"I could play the harp?" Jacqueline offered. Michel scoffed at the notion.

"That's alright, dear, one event will do," Helene said, dismissing her daughter. "Grace wants to perform again, so she shall perform again."

"I'm looking forward to it," Grace beamed. She flashed a bright smile at Jacqueline, who sent a strained one back.

***

Later in the day, Grace and Jacqueline sat outside together, enjoying the fresh, scented air the blossoming roses outside the west wing of the Hustan gave them. The two companions overlooked a bustling town area where the

23

Arisclan civilians went about their working lives. Grace could not help but think of how much calmer and more efficient the people were in this part of the land in comparison to her native clan.

"Watching your people go about their lives is like watching a colony of worker ants," Grace joked.

"As opposed to the swarms of bees that make up the people of your land," Jacqueline joked back.

"Which is why I spend more time here than over there," Grace laughed.

"I wouldn't have it any other way," Jacqueline said. Grace met her friend with a measured, studying look.

"I'll have to return to my bee-swarm-infested land soon," Grace said. "I'm to visit my siblings."

"You don't seem to want to visit them often," Jacqueline commented. "What's the occasion?"

"Sometimes we like to meet with each other on the anniversary of the death of our parents, which is only a few days from now," Grace sighed.

She did not like to talk about or even think about her late parents. Their father, Kingsley, was a passionate warrior, yet he died a mundane death of over-exhaustion caused by the stresses of anxiety and overworking a few years prior. Their mother, Faith, died a few weeks following her husband's death from the grief it caused.

"Oh, right, I'm sorry to hear that," Jacqueline condoled. A long silence held between the two of them as Grace stared over the hills of the horizon.

"I won't be here for a few weeks," she said, breaking the silence again.

"When will I see you next?" Jacqueline asked.

"At your clan's gala," Grace answered proudly. "You'll see a whole lot of me as I dazzle your people on stage."

Jacqueline nodded. "I can't wait," she said, that strained smile occupying her face again.

***

Grace travelled in the rear of a spacious, wooden-framed carriage with a velvet roof over her head, cushioned seats below her, and a man riding a domesticated lion drawing it forward. She could sense they were soon to reach their destination. A small partition of the maroon curtains that draped from the roof allowed her to confirm. They were back in her family's land.

The carriage rocked slightly, the roads made of cobbled dried mud causing trouble for its wheels. The smoothness of her journey thus far had been interrupted in more ways than one. As they passed through the village, her ears were bombarded by the sounds of the haggling merchants and unruly children who populated the streets. The air stank of alcohol and vomit as they passed by the taverns. On multiple occasions, she would hear the roars of the lion followed by the complaint of an intoxicated villager who accidentally stumbled into the carriage's path. That, as well as the overall sights of the village fronts, made her less eager to be home with each passing second.

The magnificent block that was the Clan Zhakkari Hustan acted as a haven, its simple, dark eloquence giving the general area a more dignified appearance by proxy. Despite its uncomplicated grandiloquence, Grace showed a complete lack of enthusiasm to be there.

***

Grace entered the main room of the Zhakkari Hustan. The floors were covered with a rough grey carpet that lay underneath a messy set of benches, stools, and equally rough sofas that decorated the living space. The black brick walls were the only organised part of the room, decorated with a framed painting of all the Zhakkari children. Her, her older brother Ezekiel, and her younger siblings, Samuel and Promise. One of them was in the room.

Samuel sat on one of the rough heirloom sofas, grinning to himself as he read a book. The grin was wiped from his face with quickness as he looked up from his page.

"Can I help you?" he asked, visibly confused as to why Grace was there.

"Rude way to greet a family member," Grace scoffed.

"You don't come back here very often, and most of the time you do, it's to gain or receive something," Samuel said. "So, I'll ask you again. Can I help you?"

Grace kissed her teeth in disbelief. "Do you genuinely not remember why I'm here today?" she asked. Her brother's blank expression answered that for her.

"The family dinner. The one where we gather on the anniversary of our parents' deaths to commemorate them. It's this week," Grace reminded him.

Samuel shut his book and rested it on his lap. "It must have slipped from my mind," he sighed, gripping a tuft of his afroed hair as he cursed himself for forgetting.

"You legitimately forgot? What a great son you are," Grace mocked.

"I've been busy with a lot of work recently," Samuel said in defence of his faux pas.

"So, the excuse is you had your head in the clouds over some inane new project of yours?" Grace chastised.

Samuel's mouth stretched into a malformed, toothy leer that she recognised from their childhood.

"I'll have you know I was in the process of doing something that matters. Something that will improve our family and land's position in this world," Samuel said haughtily. "Unlike you, a girl who seems intent on prancing around like a pampered socialite and pretending she's a part of a different clan."

Grace laughed, though not out of amusement. This was a clear attempt to keep control of the rising volcanic anger that was erupting inside her.

"My connection to the Bello family has been nothing but a total positive for us. Because of it, higher clans are more likely to come to our land and bless our people with gifts. Because of it, I'll be leading the festivities at *another* Arisclan gala," Grace boasted. "Over the past few years, I'd say I've done more to bring attention, status, and gold to Commonsclan Zhakkari than any plan or project your so-called *intelligent mind* has come up with."

Samuel felt a pang of pain in his heart, her words cutting deep. He thought of mentioning his likelihood of being placed on the Kingsclan Shared Council by William Khoza as a comeback. He decided to save that for later.

"Feel free to make yourself at home again," Samuel said, walking away from her with an affable expression.

Grace watched him leave the room without an extra word. She was confused by the lack of a scathing insult or disparaging remark from her younger brother to the point of concern.

***

After arranging her belongings in her old room, Grace left the Hustan in search of her brother. Though she enjoyed the teasing, insulting back-and-forth banter the two of them would have, at times, they went too far. She was unsure as to whether she had truly upset him this time around.

As Grace walked down to the village front, she found her brother amongst the civilians of the general area. The village's people were observing something with anxious excitement. Many swarmed in an unorganised fashion outside a hut, pushing, pulling, clawing, and scratching at each other. They boomed and bellowed as they watched two middle-aged women engaged in a desperate, feral attempt to kill one another. Grace pushed herself to the front of the crowd. Samuel was there, watching on in frozen horror. The women were savaging each other in a manner that even wild beasts would consider brutal.

One of these women was stout and leather-skinned with blood leaking profusely out of an eye socket that had just been gouged empty. The other was a more muscular yet slimmer woman with a shaved head and a chunk of flesh that had been ripped out of her shoulder with the marks of human teeth. The two Zhakkari siblings could not stomach the sight as the woman dug their nails into each other as if in a competition to see who could tear skin from bones first.

"What on all holy lands is happening?!" Grace asked.

"I have no idea," Samuel muttered.

Grace turned to the person next to her in the onlooking crowd. "What are they fighting so savagely over?" she asked an older man in farmer's garbs.

The man groaned as if a weight had been placed on his shoulders. He pointed towards the stout woman in the fight. She was cutting at the slimmer woman's mouth, drawing blood in an effort to force a bladed stone down her throat.

"*She* is a mother of a young child, but also a notorious drunk. So much so that she often neglects her child, sometimes for days on end," he explained.

He then pointed to the muscular woman who had spat the rock out and picked it up for herself, using it to carve at the skin on the forehead of the other woman.

"The mother had asked *her*, her neighbour, to take care of her child whilst she was out on a drunken adventure," the farmer continued. "The neighbour did a poor job of taking care of the child. She let him wander around her house until he injured himself while playing with kitchen blades."

"Is the child alright?" Grace asked.

"To an extent. He's alive but had to have his foot amputated," the man told them. "He's living in a home for discarded children in an Arisclan now."

"Horrible," Samuel uttered.

Grace nodded in sour agreement. Having seen enough, she left, pushing back through the crowd on her way to the Hustan. Samuel, on the other hand, had his eyes glued to the scene as if there was no other choice but to watch.

The fight was coming to a gruesome conclusion. The stout mother gained the upper hand, smashing her neighbour's teeth in with a mailed fist. She headbutted the muscular woman, pressing her forehead down. Her instincts took over as she bit into the woman's nose. With animalistic force, she chewed until the nose was torn off.

Even after the woman's nose was torn off in a fit of wails, the mother continued to chew at her opponent's face, a spiritual big cat gnawing at its prey.

Afterwards, she pounded what remained of the woman's face like it was a stubborn yam, leaving it in red bloody chunks similar to a rotten stew. She let out the scream of a hulking brute. Some onlookers cursed her, some cheered her on. Samuel just stood there.

The negligent mother's blood-curdling victory shouts were cut abruptly. Though she won her battle, she would not keep her life. An arrow, sharp and swift, made its way through the front of her forehead and out of the back of her head expeditiously. She gasped in shock, feeling the perfectly circular gash that had been formed through her. She dropped dead, landing over the woman she had slain. The gathered villagers muttered in confusion as they looked for who had slain her. Grace stood from afar with a quiver on her back, a bow in her hand, and a tenseness about her.

"Go home! Now!" Grace ordered as she re-joined them. The village people obliged. With the spectacle over and a direct order from one of their clan leaders, they left with their heads collectively hung as they cleared the area. They went to perform their usual monotonous village tasks as Grace glared at her brother.

"You should have called one of our Hustan defenders," Samuel said. "It's ill-suited for us as clan leaders to kill even unruly civilians in public."

"Was it not ill-suited for you to stand and watch as if you were a powerless child?" Grace asked.

Samuel had no answer for her. A mixture of morbid curiosity and an unwillingness to involve himself in such violence left him unable to do anything but watch.

Grace scoffed at her brother. "If *this* is how you lead the clan when the rest of us are gone, then perhaps you're right. Perhaps I *should* be around more."

Grace marched away from her brother, not regretting this scathing comment as opposed to the others.

Samuel seethed as he watched her leave in contempt.

A DERISIVE DINNER

EZEKIEL Zhakkari was an expert in brutality. Nothing suited him more than carving through any man who lacked the foresight to avoid him in open combat. The oldest Zhakkari child certainly looked the part of a warrior of their family. Tall, muscle-bound, bearded, and with the hair on his eyebrows thicker than the hair on his head, which he opted to shave clean.

Ezekiel sported his Clan Zhakkari battle armour with specially-manufactured scabbards fit to host a greater size and quantity of weaponry. He wielded a longsword, a two-pronged shortsword, and a battle-axe.

He and his rank of Civcaz warriors bravely threw themselves into a vicious conflict against an army of tattooed men who wore tattered blue cloth and wielded cutlasses. The Saxe-Barbarians were notorious for being lawless men of the seas. Therefore, their occupation of dry Civcaz land was bound to end in bloodshed. Bloodshed that Ezekiel was more than happy to delve into.

Ezekiel dug deep footprints in the desert sands below him as a Saxe-Barbarian rushed forward. He had just watched the wiry cutlass-wielder strike one man, cut down another, and come for him. Ezekiel braced himself as the erratic barbarian reached striking distance. He performed the most emphatic, seamless slash of an axe, connecting with his neck and sliding through it like a soft cake until the head was separated. He smiled as his decapitated opponent crashed to the floor.

Hearing only the swish of a blade through the air, Ezekiel dodged a strike from another barbarian who attempted to catch him off guard. Too little, too late. Now aware of his presence, Ezekiel evaded the next attack. With a mixture of brute strength and finesse, he caught the Saxe-Barbarian's cutlass between the blade and the handle of his axe. He pulled the barbarian towards him, unsheathed his two-pronged shortsword, and buried it in the man's eye with one rapid, impressive motion.

Ezekiel chuckled as he stared into the barbarian's one good eye, greatly amused by the tears that accompanied the whimpers of pain.

***

After the battle's conclusion, a celebration was in order. A tavern was turned upside down and inside out, no longer populated with the usual drunken patrons but with warriors in armour still covered in blood and the dancing half-naked women that accompanied them. The echoed noise of zealous celebrations bounced off all the stone walls in the establishment. Laughs, shouts, moans, and screams. It was a wonder how no one had grown deaf simply from being in attendance. The warriors and their women ran rampant.

Ezekiel sat as a king in the middle of it all, his table a throne with one of these women sitting on his lap and licking his neck as if it were the sweetest nectar.

He grabbed the teasing woman by the hair, to which she giggled in anticipation. He stared at her with intense eyes and impressed a fervent kiss on her lips. The two of them brushed their lips against one another feverishly before breaking off. She smirked at Ezekiel and went on to pursue another woman for him, as was the custom at these events.

Though Ezekiel did not wait for her return. He rose from his jagged tavern throne and wandered outside.

***

Though he often revelled in the unrestrained ardour of his fellow warriors, Ezekiel needed the occasional break. He walked away from the main thoroughfare that was the streets outside the tavern and found peace by a barn in the adjacent village. He enjoyed looking at the moon, feeling calm and undisturbed. For that moment, at least.

"Savage!" an insult Ezekiel heard levied at him. His face immediately soured, his peace disturbed as he looked to see who had spoken it. Only one other man was in the general vicinity. A lanky, weak-chinned, sullen-faced man.

"Excuse me?" Ezekiel mumbled.

"You heard what I said! You're savages! You and your warrior clan!" the man exclaimed.

Ezekiel leaned away from the barn. The man trembled slightly as the firstborn Zhakkari slowly approached him.

"Do you mean that?" Ezekiel asked him in a low voice. The lanky man gulped. He built up the resolution to continue standing his ground, raising his recessed chin upwards to force a brave stance. "I don't see why the people of this land insist on celebrating men like *you*," he critiqued.

Ezekiel looked him up and down in derisive laughter.

"And who should they celebrate instead? Men like *you*?" he asked, mocking his tone.

"Yes, they should," the lanky man insisted. "Honest working men. Those of us with a capacity for intelligence and honour, not brutality. Not you glorified thugs."

33

"Glorified thugs?" Ezekiel asked, his voice lowering in further condemnation.

"Barbarians even," the lanky doubled down.

Ezekiel laughed. "I think you're confused. The barbarians are the ones we fight to keep off this land," he growled, prodding the man's chest. "If it wasn't for savages like me, you wouldn't know the privilege of even having this conversation, you stupid fucking bastard."

The man stared at the finger poking at his chest. He grew braver by the second, invigorated by anger.

"Every time you win a battle, you and your men terrorise these villages! Turning them upside down with your wine, women, and woeful acts of *celebration*!" he shouted. "You're violent and crude! The only difference between you and those Saxe-Barbarians is that they travel by sea and you by land!"

Ezekiel lowered his head, his eyes seeming to darken as he studied the man's face. "Then why don't I show you just how much of a barbarian I am?" he asked with laughter.

The lanky man's eyes widened in shock. What he last saw that night was Ezekiel's bruised knuckles as they clattered into his face. One blow to render him unconscious.

"This is what you're doing instead of the women at our tavern? Harassing locals?" a familiar voice said to him.

Ezekiel saw a handsome, cheerful-faced young man approach him. The man wore the same battle armour, only his scabbards were filled with two shortswords and a spear with a heavy blade. These were the weapons featured on the Arisclan Rashid emblem on his armour's chest.

"I don't punch people without reason, Ibrahim," Ezekiel responded. "You should have heard the verbal manure he was spewing."

"I heard some of it. I don't blame you for beating him, but I would have taken a much more diplomatic approach, to be honest," Ibrahim laughed.

Ezekiel scoffed. "Have you been enhancing your soul's justness virtue recently?"

"No. However, I think you should, as well as your ingenuity. Perhaps there wouldn't be an unconscious villager at our feet if you had," Ibrahim mocked.

"Your father didn't recruit me for the Clan Rashid Warrior Ranks for my soul's justness or ingenuity, but for its vitality," Ezekiel argued. He pointed down to the unconscious man. "That right there is the type of drawback that comes with such a decision."

Ibrahim shook his head. "Very well, let's return to the tavern. Those women aren't going to fuck themselves."

Ezekiel laughed, Ibrahim joining him with chuckles. The eldest Zhakkari was not one to keep many friends, but the oldest son of Arisclan Rashid was an exception. He was amused by Ibrahim's flippant attitude.

For the time being, at least.

***

A few days following the battle against the barbarians and the wild events that followed it, Ezekiel was far from Arisclan Rashid's land. He enjoyed feeling the rougher grounds and breathing the lower-quality air that came with arrival on Clan Zhakkari land. With a saddle and rope, he rode a domesticated lion to the front entrance of the family's Hustan as the defenders escorted him in.

Having settled his lion, chaining it in the indoor yard, he ventured to the front room of their Hustan and sat in the first old chair he could find. Instead of going out of his way to greet his siblings, he found himself too drained from the journey and sat there, waiting for them to show.

"Afternoon, Ezekiel," Samuel greeted, the first person to show as he entered the room. Ezekiel stood up to greet his brother with a handshake.

"Is everyone here for the commemorative dinner?" Ezekiel asked.

"Grace is here. Promise is yet to arrive," Samuel answered.

As if the mere utterance of her name summoned her, Grace entered the room. For the first time in forever, three Zhakkari siblings occupied the front room of the Hustan, standing in between the clutter of paintings, scrolls, and weathered seats.

" I can't remember the last time I saw both my brothers at once," Grace said, commenting on the phenomenon.

"Far from the old days when we'd train in the yard under mother's supervision and father's orders," Samuel said. His brother scoffed.

"When *we* used to train," Ezekiel corrected, gesturing towards Grace, who looked down on him, too. Samuel rolled his eyes at both.

"Yes, you're right, I wasn't focused when it came to the physical trials. But I was twice as excellent when it came to the mental trials," Samuel retorted. "That's why I surpassed the rest of you by a nation mile."

"Speak for the others. You didn't surpass me by a mile in any nation," Grace said. "I, for one, was certainly clever enough to almost keep up with you when it came to reading and writing."

"Only because of your obsession with competing with me. Which you only started doing once you realised that you'd never be able to compete with Ezekiel's strength as a woman," Samuel laughed.

"Which is why you're second to us in both areas, but not first in anything," Ezekiel added, mockingly.

Grace groaned. She hated it when her brothers would team up against her. "That just means I'm more well-rounded, doesn't it? That's why I earn the most gold and favour out of all of us nowadays, isn't it?" Grace gloated. Ezekiel grunted, forcing a grin away. Samuel raised his eyebrows. Neither had a retort.

"You're all arguing already?" laughed a soothing feminine voice. The three of them looked towards the room's entrance to see their youngest sibling, Promise. With her there, the Zhakkari sibling quartet was complete.

"You're finally here," Samuel said, smiling.

Grace and Ezekiel also greeted her with warm smiles. With her perfectly braided hair, spotless skin, and light white teeth, Promise's presence seemed capable of calming anyone down, even her arguing siblings.

"Nice to see you again, Promise," Ezekiel said, greeting her with a gripping, loving embrace that he had not even thought to offer Samuel or Grace. Grace also embraced Promise with a hug afterwards. It seemed that whatever vitriol the siblings had for each other was put aside when it came to her, the perpetual baby of the family.

"Mother and father would love this," Promise said. "The four of us still meeting to honour their passing. Even with all the different paths we took in life."

"Yeah, different paths," Grace scoffed in Samuel's direction. He rolled his eyes at her again.

"We should start the dinner," Samuel suggested.

***

The disordered Clan Zhakkari dining room had been cleared. The four siblings stood on either side of a long table constructed from a blend of iroko and mahogany wood.

In front of them were bowls with simple meals of dark meat, sweet bread, and fresh water. None of them had taken a bite of food yet. With their eyes closed, arms clasped together, and muscles tensed ardently, they performed a ritualistic prayer.

"...vitality, ingenuity, regality, justness. We ask you all to be with us in essence, reverberating through our souls with the spirits of our late mother and father, from now until the end of our lives," Ezekiel said, concluding the prayer. With that done, they could sit down and eat.

The dinner was quiet for a while, with the siblings eating their food in sanctimonious silence. Promise, however, could not contain herself for long.

"I have exciting news to share with you three," she blurted out giddily. Ezekiel, Grace, and Samuel's eyes darted towards her.

"What is it?" Grace asked.

Promise outstretched her hand. On her ring finger was a ribbon that, if it were tied any tighter, would have cut off the circulation to her hand. The ribbon featured a logo depicting a winding, flowing river. The emblem of Arisclan Irie.

"It's been over a year since my marriage to Francis and the birth of our baby," Promise reminded them. "Meaning I am officially considered an honorary member of Clan Irie, entitling me to a portion of their land!"

The faces of her siblings lit up, each with a combination of elation and envy. Samuel started a congratulatory round of applause, to which Grace and Ezekiel echoed.

"Congratulations, sister," Ezekiel said. She thanked him with a bow. Ezekiel thought about Promise's husband, Francis Irie. He had only met him a few times, but had already decided he did not care much for the man. He saw him as being too meek, yet at the same time, too righteous.

The fact that he treated Promise well and made her happy enough to bear his child was enough justification for Ezekiel to have no real problem with him. That and the revelation that he had given her land was enough to decide that Francis Irie was not too bad.

"Do you know what this fantastic news means?" Grace asked. Samuel saw the smile on her face, anticipating what she was to comment on. "It means that Samuel is the only Zhakkari sibling not to be connected to an Arisclan in any way. How unfortunate," she chuckled.

Ezekiel chortled at his sister's jest. Promise grinned awkwardly, not sure if it would be right to laugh. Samuel did not seem to take offence, much to everyone's surprise. He nodded in non-verbal confirmation of the statement.

"You're right. With your strong ties to Clan Bello, Ezekiel's fighting in the Clan Rashid Warrior Ranks, and Promise being an honorary member of Clan Irie due to her husband and child, it seems I am the only one without the privilege of being connected to an Arisclan," Samuel detailed. "But I think you'll find that what I *am* connected to is even better."

"And what's that?" Grace asked.

Samuel stood in the manner a royal would when giving a speech to his people. "My fair siblings, it is with great pleasure that I inform you are currently in the presence of the newest member of the Shared Kingsclan Council."

The faces that Promise's news prompted returned in an exaggerated fashion. With their mouths agape in momentary speechlessness, Samuel bathed in the ego-validation that came with the looks of shock and awe from his siblings.

"Seriously?" Promise gasped.

"I've heard you talk about all that, but I didn't think you'd manage it!" Ezekiel said, letting out a booming laugh heartier than the meal in front of him. "Well fucking done!"

Samuel nodded downwards in appreciation of both. He glanced at Grace, who he could tell was simmering with begrudging respect.

"Well done," she said reluctantly. "Quite the achievement."

"And I didn't have to latch myself onto another family's gala events to achieve it," Samuel added, not able to resist using the upper hand he now had. Grace's eyes narrowed at him. She glowered at his smug face, bubbling with frustration.

"Don't get cocky. You might have the power to change the lands now, but you certainly don't have the ability to do so," Grace insulted. "Especially if how you handled that gruesome situation the other day is how you're going to handle similar ones in the future."

"Gruesome situation?" Ezekiel asked.

Samuel sat in his seat with a dejected sigh. He would have preferred that situation to be forgotten. It brought his spirits right back down to the core of the earth.

"Two women were mauling each other to the point of eyes being gouged and noses being torn, and *no one* bothered to try and stop them. Some of the villagers even gathered around to cheer them on!" Grace complained. "One of the women had her face bashed into a bloody paste," she said.

"Lord," Promise gasped, covering her mouth and nose. Ezekiel's face twisted.

"And during it all, Samuel watched with the rest of the villagers, doing nothing until I intervened," Grace said. Samuel sent her an evil-eyed scowl. She returned the gesture, creating an intense energy in the room for a while.

Shortly after, Samuel stormed out of the dining area, having not even touched his meal. In his absence, the coarse atmosphere coarsened ever more.

Promise twiddled her thumbs, her insides churning with discomfort. The news of the two women disturbed Ezekiel also. Though, in a way he could have never anticipated.

Gruesome events of that nature were not ones to bother him since he had seen and done similar actions in battle. But hearing that something like that happened in the middle of one of their villages was a different story. He often thought about how certain people would talk about how the land was degenerating both physically and in terms of the culture of their people. He remembered how he used to overhear his parents worry about such a thing happening when he would eavesdrop on their conversations growing up. How it could doom their clan and their land as a whole.

Ezekiel always dismissed these parental concerns as fearmongering. He saw it as the excuse they used to justify the nonstop training and schooling. What if it was not?

Taking the story of the fighting women into account, it became clear that warriors of his calibre were not the only Zhakkari-folk who were becoming savage and barbaric.

A COUPLE'S BLOOD

PROMISE Zhakkari spent every hour of the morning cuddling her baby with not a single desire in her heart to do anything else. She gushed as she hugged the plump infant boy, pressing his face to hers as he babbled. Her bed acted as their sanctuary. Flowery pink curtains hung from the ceiling, draping over them from all sides. Their fluorescent beauty shielded her and her sweet boy from the world.

An outside force broke into their little world. But a welcome one at that. The curtains parted, and the cheerful face of a young man with a thick, neatly-trimmed moustache entered. Promise's husband's face was enough to fill her heart with thumping joy and send her baby into a fit of giggles. Francis joined his wife and baby in their pink sanctuary, feeling as if he were the luckiest man in all of Civcaz.

***

Afternoon came, and the room was quieter. Their baby had been put to bed, his peaceful snores creating a soothing ambience. Francis sat in a rocking chair marked with carvings of Clan Irie river symbols, the head of his chair brushing against the pink curtains. Promise sat a few paces away from him on a flat embroidered cushion, facing the fireplace with her hands clasped and eyes closed. Francis lowered the novel he was reading with a bemused grin.

"Are you worshipping the four virtues?" Francis laughed.

"Yes," Promise answered, an air of confusion about her as she opened their eyes. "Why is that funny?"

"It isn't. You just look adorably sweet, that's all," Francis complimented.

Promise parted a hand through hair that was as warm and fuzzy as the feelings swelling in her heart.

"It's also strange to see. You're one of the only people I know who still regularly worships the virtues."

"So does my family. Doesn't yours?" Promise asked.

"Not necessarily," Francis answered.

"Don't you want the virtues to hold firm in your soul?" Promise questioned, concerned.

Francis tapped his book on his lap. "I understand the need for justness in the soul, but I'm not so sure about ingenuity, regality, and vitality," he argued. "I've often seen people use them as excuses for their heinous acts. Especially vitality. I've seen the worst excused through that alone."

Promise's mind flashed to what Grace told them the other night. She thought of the woman who tore the face of her neighbour. The memory caused her breakfast to do somersaults in her stomach.

"I see your point," Promise said, unclasping her hands.

***

Promise cradled her sleeping baby in a fluffy blanket, carefully holding him as she rode in an open-roofed carriage. Her husband sat beside her, wearing Clan Irie armour despite not being a warrior. This was the same armour worn by the two Hustan defenders whose lions

43

carried them through the land. The Clan Irie servants took them on a scenic route, their lions purring as they traversed the Irie River.

Promise watched in fascination as women of the village collected water in buckets, then carried them in stacks on their heads to bring to the men on the mainland.

"That's an interesting sight," Francis commented.

"I know. It's beautiful," Promise gushed.

"That's not how I'd describe it," Francis said.

Promise realised Francis was looking elsewhere. She turned in the direction of his gaze.

Far off in the distance, she saw a dispute of law and order. Kingsclan Khoza warriors were arresting a man dressed in cloaks and precious jewels, dragging him by the heel out of the grasslands and into stone territory. She could faintly see the blood from his head leave a trail across the grass as he was forced off the land.

"What's happening? What did he do?" Promise asked.

"I believe I know that man," Francis said as he squinted his eyes. "If he's who I think he is, he's being exiled for his haughtiness."

Promise scrunched her nose in confusion. "How so?"

"That man became very rich by buying and selling wares at the marketplace. He thought that meant he could buy a portion of land reserved for Kingsclans. I'm sure he regrets his choices now," said Francis.

Promise saw the man mouth pleas of mercy, his back staining the stones he was hauled over with his thick dark blood. She looked away.

***

Samuel was surrounded by pearly white columns that shot up from either side of him to a ceiling one hundred feet high. He walked down a grey marble floor towards a door.

44

He approached it with excited purpose, stopping in his tracks as soon as he was there. He took a deep breath, psyching himself up before finally opening it and entering.

The room was vast yet mostly empty, the only point of focus being an octagonal meeting table of a refined, soft-metallic consistency. Sitting around the table were each member of the Shared Kingsclan Council, all members of higher Civcaz society that he could recognise anywhere.

Samuel took a seat. Across from him was William of Kingsclan Khoza, the somewhat stuffy man who granted him his seat on the council. Sitting to his left and right were two men. The first was Robert Khoza, his brother, silent in speech and hulking in size. The second was Patrick Cele, a short, stubby, fresh-faced man whom Samuel knew to be a former worship leader at the temples of soul. Next to them on either side were the thick-browed twins, Katherine and Kaya Amara, also former worship leaders. Finally, the last two members of the council were from Kingsclan Osei, their clothes proving they were the richest and most powerful clan in the land.

Florence Osei's hair was decorated with neon green gems interlocked with her braids and clashing against a silk black dress. Her husband wore Civcaz warrior armour that was ornate with the same stones, including the emblem of a crown hung over the top of an ancient staff. These garbs were fit for the most influential man in all the lands, Christian Osei.

"Welcome to the council, Samuel Zhakkari," Christian greeted in a warm and dignified manner.

"I'm very happy to be here, Osei sir," Samuel said. He gave a nod to every member of the council, a sign of respect they returned.

"Right," William Khoza said, clearing his throat as his fingers wrapped against the table. "Let's settle this week's matters."

***

Samuel had only been on the Shared Kingsclan Council for just over two hours, yet he was already starting to become disillusioned. When he dreamed of having a place here as a child, he imagined he would be discussing the most pressing matters in Civcaz with the most intelligent and influential people in the land. That had not been the case so far.

"And we're all in agreement over the fact that Clan Godwin should have their village stock depleted by seven percent this winter as punishment for their past actions, as well as our decision to use them as reparation stock for the other clans?" William proposed. The other council members tilted their heads upwards. Samuel reluctantly copied.

The council spent a considerable amount of time discussing different ways to punish Clan Godwin, from cutting off and redistributing parts of their land to planning an exhibition exile for any people of the land who spoke out against this. Samuel was no stranger to Civcaz's disdain for the Godwins due to the family's conquering past, but he did not know it was to this extent. It came to the point where Samuel started to root for the Godwins out of spite.

"The next matter to discuss is the handling of John Godwin's remains," William continued. "His family want him to be buried on the same grounds as the other late clan leaders, but I cannot in good conscience allow his corpse to soil the earth of-"

"Are we only discussing policies that involve punishing Clan Godwin?!" Samuel exclaimed in frustration.

As soon as the words had left his mouth, he was struck with the sense that he had said something deeply wrong.

Almost every set of eyes shot daggers into his mind and heart. He felt a sudden animosity from all directions.

William Khoza scowled at him the hardest. He opened his mouth, no doubt in preparation to scold Samuel. He was prevented from doing so by Christian. The Kingsclan Osei leader smiled, raising an index finger.

"He's right, let's move on to the next set of topics," Christian recommended. "Amara twins. You said you had a proposal planned earlier?"

Katherine and Kaya furrowed their heavy eyebrows, sharing a glance before speaking.

"We're looking to shut down another set of worship temples in the mainland," Katherine said.

"We'll repurpose the buildings as tavern pleasure brothels. The people there seem to be in use of them the most," Kaya added.

Patrick Cele rubbed his chin in contemplation. "I'm not sure about brothels, but I do like the sound of repurposing the temples. What about new exotic food markets?"

"That's a reasonable proposal. Either way, the temples should be destroyed and put to better use," Katherine said. Kaya huffed a breath in corroboration.

"Yes, I like that idea," agreed Florence.

"Are we all in agreement that a portion of the worship temples in the mainland should be repurposed?" Christian Osei asked.

All the council members tilted their heads back in agreement. All apart from Samuel. Once again, he felt the heat of animosity rest upon his body as scowling eyes were directed at him.

"You disagree, Samuel?" Christian asked.

"Wholeheartedly. The temples have been kept the way they are for a good reason," Samuel answered.

"And what reason is that?" William asked, regretting having offered Samuel the role on the council.

"I believe that question answers itself. The numbers may have severely decreased over the years, but there are still many who worship the four virtues," Samuel argued. "Why would you destroy the main place where they can practice their faith?"

Samuel expected at least one other member of the council to share his grievances. Not a single person budged in his favour.

"The four virtues," Florence scoffed.

Christian smiled at his wife wryly. "Do you have an opinion you'd like to share, sweetheart?"

"I think putting stock in those virtues as a way to live your life is unnecessary. Antiquated, even," Florence said.

Samuel was taken aback by this sentiment. But not as taken aback as he would be by the sentiments that followed.

"If I'm to be completely honest, I've developed that view of the four virtues myself, too," Patrick Cele said. "They're old ideals that could be said to do more harm than good nowadays."

"If anything, you could argue they're completely out of place in today's society," Kaya added. Katherine grunted in agreement.

"Yes, that's right. I think it would be best if we adopted a societal model that didn't incorporate them at all," William agreed. "An overreliance on those virtues could one day cause this land to fall."

Samuel could not believe what he was hearing. "I couldn't disagree more! It's the lack of those virtues that *is* causing our land to fall today!" he retorted to the room as a whole. "In fact, I was going to suggest implementing policies that can teach the youth the way to enhance all virtues in their soul to prevent said fall!"

The council members shared looks of distaste and disregard. Of the many types of reactions to his policy proposals that Samuel had once envisioned, this was the one he least anticipated.

He found it particularly peculiar how William Khoza was acting as if he opposed them when his reaction to the same beliefs during their interview meeting was positive. Samuel looked around the table in astonished confusion.

"While I appreciate the passion you have for the four virtues, I *am* concerned about the place where it's coming from," Christian Osei said. "Need I remind you that it is the same vehement fixation on them that Clan Godwin used to excuse their past crimes?"

Judging glares from the other council members told Samuel they shared the same belief.

He knew when to cut his losses. With a resigned sigh, he sat down and stayed quiet.

***

The council meeting concluded an hour later. An entire hour in which Samuel did not speak, lest he be met with more animosity and accusation. As he and the other members poured out of the room in agreement on all issues and policies that had been brought up in the meantime, Samuel found himself twice as disillusioned with the state of the council, the land, and his life.

"Don't fret, young man," Christian Osei advised as he walked past him with a smile. "You'll adjust to the culture of these meetings over time."

"Yes. Of course, sir," Samuel sighed back.

***

"What are you thinking about?" Francis asked Promise as they lay cuddling in bed that night. With the baby being looked after by maids, they snuggled up against each other in a sensual embrace. Instead of enjoying their moment alone, Promise stared off into space.

"What are you thinking? Tell me," Francis urged softly. Promise sighed. "My mind is racing with the tales my older siblings were telling me about the other day. About how the land is degenerating. Nonsense like that," she said, pre-emptively dismissing her worries as she verbalised them. This was a bad habit of hers.

Francis laughed. "It's not good to worry, my dear. You must trust that all will be fine," he said.

"Yes," she uttered in response.

But Promise could not stop worrying, despite how much she wanted to. She felt as if she had no choice but to worry. Something was altering the Land of Civcaz. Something deeply negative was changing the land and its people.

She did not know what it was, but she could feel its sensation eating away at her heart and soul.

A REPUTATION SOILED

SAMUEL Zhakkari was not enjoying his new status as a member of the Shared Kingsclan Council nearly as much as he wished to. Though it did have some perks.

He was granted a room within the stratagem-quarters and a cosy one at that. This room had a bed fit for a king with thick animal fur duvets and shelves carved into the pristine white stone walls to host his mountains of novels, tomes, and scrolls.

Samuel hardly enjoyed the perks of this cushy room. He sat on the floor drinking his dozenth chalice of wine, even though it was the middle of the day. He took another careless sip from his chalice, staining his black Zhakkari robes with the remnants of a dark purple drink. To lift his spirits and stir his creative juices, Samuel chose to indulge in pleasures he had denied himself in the lead-up to his council introduction. It had been a while since he had indulged in alcohol or women. He still had half a chalice full of one and was rifling through his pocket for gold coins so he could obtain the other.

A gentle knock was heard at his door. Samuel put down the chalice and wiped his mouth clean. He groaned as he rose to answer.

It was as if someone had read his mind and heard his need for a woman, as one appeared at his doorstep. She was a woman he thoroughly enjoyed the look of, a lady of short yet svelte figure with a head of vibrant curly hair. The type of woman he would have purchased *favours* from during his more unscrupulous days.

"Samuel Zhakkari of the Shared Kingsclan Council?" she said as if she were not sure.

Samuel did not confirm or deny. He only stared forward and smiled politely. His politeness was both unreciprocated and flouted with violence.

The svelte woman grabbed his neck. She dug in her nails until they drew blood redder than their coating. Samuel's body convulsed as he took her hand in a constricted attempt to pry himself free. With her grip confining his neck, the woman pushed herself into the room, shutting the door behind her with another hand. She scratched hard, leaving a shallow yet bleeding mark on Samuel's throat as he fell to the carpeting on the floor.

"What in all souls are you doing?" Samuel asked, gasping for air, and crawling away from her with a hand over the bloody scar on his neck.

The woman ignored his question, marching forward in silence as if she had a mission to complete. She lifted her dress to expose a gorgeous, toned midriff that had a hidden scabbard tied around it. She equipped a blade that bore a similar appearance to the traditional two-pronged dagger of Clan Zhakkari.

"Help! Somebody! There's a madwoman with a blade!" Samuel bellowed at the top of his lungs, his voice echoing through the room. No one in the general vicinity was listening. He leapt upwards to escape, but was knocked down as the blade-wielding mistress lunged at him.

Samuel struggled to keep the blade away from his throat as the woman wrestled him, determined to cut it.

"Who are you? Why do you so desperately want me dead?!" Samuel exclaimed during the struggle. He received no answers, only cuts from the knife being dragged against his hands as he held it away from his neck.

Samuel was not a violent man. Unlike Ezekiel, who revelled in it, and Grace, who indulged when necessary, he was more like his sister Promise, having no skill for it at all. Regardless, his instincts from the little physical schooling he did growing up had kicked in.

He bashed the woman's skull with a headbutt, disorientating her enough for him to push her off. She was quick to crawl back upwards, but just as quick to fall again as Samuel struck her with a swinging kick to her throat. She clasped her throat, choking and coughing as he reached for her dropped blade.

The svelte woman swivelled towards Samuel to retrieve her knife. As she bounded towards him, he bounded towards her. He cut two jagged slashes, a vertical one down her lips as a product of his inaccuracy, and a horizontal one across her throat, where he met his target.

She convulsed, squirming on the floor as blood leaked out from her mouth and neck.

As a safety measure, Samuel stabbed her multiple times in the gut, over and over in the same spot, until he felt no movement. He released the deepest, most stressed of breaths as he discarded the blade and lay there in exhaustion.

Samuel looked up from her body to see that the door was open. Two stern defenders decked in sturdy Kingsclan armour were marching in.

"Where were you when you were needed? She almost killed me!" Samuel exclaimed to the two men in gasping breaths. He collected himself, taking a deep breath. "Anyways, thank the virtues you're here. I wouldn't know where to start when it comes to cleaning this bloody mess."

The quarters-defenders stared at each other for a moment as they stopped in front of him, then back at Samuel. They spoke curtly.

"Samuel Zhakkari. You are being detained for the assault and murder of a Kingsclan pleasure-maiden," the defender to the right informed.

Samuel's mouth contorted in confusion. "No, you're mistaken. I was the one being attacked in the first place."

The defenders shook their heads in unison. "I don't think we've misunderstood *anything*," the defender to the left of him said.

Samuel watched in disbelief as the guards closed in on him, their glistening weapons readied. A slower mind would have stayed frozen in confusion. Samuel realised what was occurring in an instant.

With the most athletic promise the scholarly Zhakkari had ever shown in his life, he shoved his way past the guards, breaking into a sprinting escape.

***

The gem adornments that hung over Grace's regal Zhakkari dress dangled as she bowed to the round of applause bestowed upon her. She had taken up a stage in the royal halls of Clan Bello, concluding a set of song and dance performances underneath the lights of purple flame chandeliers. Crowds of distinguished ladies and gentlemen celebrated her very being.

As Grace stepped off the stage, the people of Clan Bello's land swarmed her, showering the second-born Zhakkari with more appreciation and gratitude, eager to get the chance to speak to or even stand beside her. They were all shooed away by members of the immediate Bello family, who sectioned her off. The parents, Simon and Helene Bello, gave her hugs of love and pride. Michel stared at her with playful, love-struck eyes. Jacqueline seemed less appreciative of Grace than the rest of her family, but still offered a smile of thanks.

"Wonderful as always, Grace!" Simon cheered with an arm around her shoulder.

"Very wonderful," Michel agreed, deep in voice. His and Grace's eyes danced in a flirtation with one another.

"Yes, very good," Jacqueline agreed, though she sounded more begrudging than celebratory.

"I swear, seeing you on that stage fills me with so much pride! It's as if you are my own daughter!" Helene celebrated. This assertion put a bad taste in the mouth of Jacqueline, her actual daughter.

"Thank you, all of you. It was a pleasure to perform for your clan again," Grace gushed with gratitude.

Simon, Michel, and Helene heaped more embraces of praise onto her. Jacqueline crossed her arms but kept her smile, growing tired of their elation yet being careful not to make her feelings obvious.

"Grace, shall we go mingle?" she offered as an excuse to take her away from her family.

"I don't see why not," Grace said.

The two women linked arms and disappeared into the crowds.

Whilst she no longer had to witness her family gushing over Grace, Jacqueline witnessed the people of her clan cornering them for conversation, with many members using any opportunity to sing Grace's praises during the event. She saw herself having to form another excuse to escape the masses. The two of them stood to the side of the room, away from everyone else's dazzled eyes.

"Crowds. Always *so* overwhelming," Jacqueline said.

"I don't find them to be so," Grace said. "If anything, I find them invigorating."

"Of course," Jacqueline uttered in quiet contempt.
Grace heard her mutters of discontent but pretended she did not. She decided it was best not to respond directly, though she planned to shed light on it irreverently.

"You know, the one negative of having all these people love me is that it complicates my marriage prospects," Grace commented. "How can I choose from so many great suitors?" she asked rhetorically.

"Quite the dilemma," Jacqueline sighed, semi-sarcastically.

"I envy you for not having this problem," Grace jibed.
Jacqueline gasped. "I receive plenty of attention from plenty of men who beg for my hand in marriage!" she protested.

"I don't mean fishermen and tavern patrons, I mean men of the highest standing," Grace said. "No offence."

"No offence was taken," Jacqueline lied through gritted teeth. The condescending smile Grace flashed set her livid. Grace was well aware of this and decided to push the mockery further.

"But of all these high-standing men, there's only one whose proposal I'd ever take seriously."

"And who's that?"

"Your brother, Michel," Grace answered with the wryest of smiles. "I've seen the way he looks at me. I think we'd go together *very* well."

Jacqueline's eyes widened. Her nostrils flared. She could no longer mask her disdain, never mind contain it. Looking into Grace's mischievous eyes and goading smile fuelled the passions of discontent that were set to explode in furious glory. Before she could release such fury, their attention was pulled elsewhere.

"Grace Zhakkari!" boomed the voice of a man. It shook her to her core. She knew that one's name being called in that tone and manner was a prelude to disaster.

Grace and Jacqueline glanced towards the entrance of the gala hall, where crowds of hundreds of Clan Bello civilians parted like a drying sea. A series of Kingsclan defenders walked through this parted sea, stomping forward as if they had been preparing for battle. These rough, burly men glared at Grace. Their leader pointed a finger at her.

"What did you do?" asked Jacqueline.

"I'm not sure," Grace said.

The defenders marched their way towards her, the crowds following their lead.

"You are being detained for the crime of aiding in a plan to murder a lady of the Kingsclan quarters that was carried out by your brother, Samuel," the lead defender informed both her and the general crowd.

"I beg your fucking pardon?!" Grace exclaimed.

"Earlier today, we detained Samuel Zhakkari for beating, raping, and murdering a pleasure-maiden in a sick act of obsessive perversion," the defender explained to both her and the people of Clan Bello. "When interrogated, he implicated you and your siblings for having helped him plan

57

the attack by organising for that specific pleasure-maiden to be sent to his doorstep."

The crowds of gala attendees gasped, startled by the news. Grace's jaw dropped so hard it threatened to snap at the joints.

"He fucking what?!" Grace screamed.

"Grace, is any of this true?!" Jacqueline asked.

"No! Fucking no!" Grace exclaimed. Though her protests sounded more petulant than absolving. Some of the gala attendees felt inclined to believe the pinned accusations.

Grace's mind was in a frazzled mess. Not a single word of accusation that was being uttered made the slightest sense to her. It was so nonsensical, she could not even think of how to defend herself.

"This is preposterous!" Simon shouted in defence. "She would never do such a thing!"

"We'd like to think so, at least," Michel added.

"She wouldn't! Our Grace wouldn't!" Helene insisted desperately.

"*Your* Grace?" Jacqueline scoffed in a whisper.
The hundreds of people at the Clan Bello gala split into an almost even crowd of rowdy panic and petulance. One half shouted in Grace's defence, echoing the sentiments of Simon and Helene. The other half believed the Kingsclan defenders, cursing her wickedness and requesting her arrest.

"They're right, I wouldn't! I have no idea where in all four virtues these accusations are coming from!" Grace said, her voice shaking.

"What about what you told me earlier? Before the gala?" Jacqueline asked.

Grace turned towards her childhood companion with snapping speed. "What?!"

"You told me something about how your brother has concerningly morbid sexual proclivities that your family struggles to keep a secret," Jacqueline lied.

A convincing enough performance for some of those at the gala to swallow.

"What? I said no such thing!" Grace shouted.

"You did. You even told me that despite how much it disgusts you, sometimes you help him obtain the women he can subject to these acts," Jacqueline said, continuing to spin her lie. "I had no idea it was to this extent, though. Allowing your kin to get off to murdering a pleasure-maiden? How disgustingly cruel."

The sound of murmurs patterned through the room as a rumour mill spread thoughts and grievances about the Zhakkari family at record speeds.

"Where the fuck did you get any of that falsified nonsense from?!" Grace berated. Jacqueline forced away a smile that was forming on her lips.

"Enough of this," the lead Kingsclan defender grunted. He grabbed hold of Grace, detaining her by force.

"Get your fucking hands off me!" Grace demanded. "People of Clan Bello, tell them to unhand me!"

No one listened. Not the Bello parents, Michel, or anyone who had been singing her praises an hour ago.

Grace saw the smug grin on Jacqueline's face as the defender seized her. "Tell them you're lying, you sour fucking bitch! Tell them! Now!" she screamed until her voice went hoarse.

Jacqueline gave Grace a condescending wave goodbye as the defenders forced her out of the gala.

***

Grace thrashed, kicked, and screamed in defiance as the Kingsclan men carried her across the Bello fields.

"Stop moving, you're only making this harder for yourself!" the defender holding her chastised. Grace took this as permission to thrash and kick harder.

The defender grunted. "If you keep this up, I'll stab you in your fucking cunt-"

With skilful hands and raw determination, Grace unsheathed a blade from the defender's armour's scabbard. No hesitation whatsoever, she sank it into his arm deep enough to completely hide the blade. The defender screamed, releasing her in pain.

Grace took the opportunity to sprint away from the defenders as the one she attacked attended to the wound that drenched his arm in blood. She rushed towards the nearest hill she could find and threw herself down it.

She tumbled down the hill, scraping and bruising every inch of skin on her arms, tearing her dress, and cutting open her cheek. Her audacious leap succeeded in its goal. There was a considerable distance between her and the defenders.

Grace ran faster than she ever had in her life, tears in her eyes. She could not begin to comprehend what was happening to her as she sprinted to hide in the first forest that she found on her escape path.

***

Much later, Grace panted as she rested her body against a tree. With her mind shattered, she struggled to piece together what was happening. She found it impossible to reach any reasonable conclusions.

She stopped thinking and gave way to tears. She felt as if she were alone and doomed. Yet she was not.

To her surprise, Grace found that her younger brother was hiding in the same forest. With cuts and bruises of his own and one eye swollen, Samuel walked to her with a face of tearful sorrow.

"You're safe. Good," he strained, his voice weak from the damage done to his neck.

Grace could not decide whether she was more relieved by his presence or aggravated by his existence.

A WARRIOR CHAINED

EZEKIEL Zhakkari's mace crashed into the chest of his opponent, winding him. The hit sealed his third tournament victory of the day as the warrior crumbled to the floor.

Ezekiel raised his weapon to the air, letting out a passionate scream that was drowned out by the cheers of those who watched. Hundreds of men sat in an arena encircling a compact sand battlefield where he stood. Amongst them was their clan leader, Ahmed Rashid, a short yet robust man who, despite his high station, wore corroded, blood-stained, and battle-hardened armour.

"Another victory for one of the best soldiers in our clan's ranks! Ezekiel *'The Animal'* Zhakkari!" Ahmed roared in an announcement to the entire arena. The civilians of Clan Rashid who had come to watch the bout surged with ferocious enthusiasm, clapping and shouting as Arisclan defenders carried Ezekiel's beaten opponent off the compacted sand grounds and into the doors on the barrier below the seating.

"And now for his final bout, and what will prove to be his hardest opponent yet! My fantastic son, Ibrahim Rashid!" he announced with great pride.

Wooden bifold doors opened from the underside of the arena stands. Ibrahim walked out of them, his armour polished, his mace in hand, and his face glistening as if he were wearing make-up. The crowds chanted his name as he approached Ezekiel in the middle of the arena. When the two men met, they bowed ceremoniously.

"Don't get upset when I win, alright?" Ibrahim laughed with a wink.

"You wish," Ezekiel scoffed.

The brothers in arms stepped away from each other. Both gripped their weapons tightly with anticipation.

"Fight!" Ahmed shouted. The two warriors did just that. Ezekiel and Ibrahim rushed towards each other with blistering speed. The sound of their maces clashing together would have echoed through the arena had the excited crowds not been exclaiming their glory.

The rules for these tournaments were simple. No strikes to the head, groin, or of a lethal enough force to be fatal. Everything else was permitted.

Ezekiel swung a strike to Ibrahim's stomach with brute strength. Ibrahim skilfully stepped out of the way. With a swivel, he struck back. Ezekiel parried his attack with his mace. Mocking him, Ibrahim performed the exact same parry move he did, down to the same placement of the feet as he drew away. Annoyed, Ezekiel sent a brutal, unrefined downward blow to Ibrahim. With a simple drop of the shoulder, Ibrahim avoided any damage and inflicted some of his own. He faked a swing of his mace with speed that Ezekiel fell for, leading to him protecting the wrong part of his body and earning a hit to the ribs.

Wasting no time in recovering, Ezekiel blindsided Ibrahim with a swift and violent return swing that was too fast to dodge, slamming his thigh. Ibrahim stayed on his feet and lunged back into battle in time for Ezekiel's next attack.

The two young men clashed maces again. Eager to get the upper hand on the other, they both sent precise strike after precise strike, desperate to catch their opponent off guard. But every time, they could only hit each other's weapons, unable to land a solid strike.

"End him already, son!" Ahmed Rashid screamed with vexed impatience.

Ibrahim chuckled. "Father knows best."
He attempted an audacious strike of graceful beauty, spinning with finesse and preparing for a final great blow. Ezekiel ducked under the blow and sent a matching one, only quicker and with less fanfare. With a powerful clubbing bash of his mace, he shot Ibrahim to the ground. Dusts of sand lifted into the air as the Rashid warrior fell with a thud.

The crowd watched with bated breath as Ibrahim attempted to stand. The blow had winded him to such an extent that he could barely bring himself up on one knee. He could no longer fight.

Roars of triumphant cheering from the arena stands confirmed Ezekiel's victory.

"I would have preferred to say this about my son, but oh well! The winner of this quarter's Rashid Tournament is Ezekiel Zhakkari!" Ahmed Rashid announced.

Ezekiel growled like a wild beast, thumping his mace against his chest as the crowd went wild.

"Don't get upset, alright?" Ezekiel echoed back to his defeated friend amusingly.

Ibrahim shook his head, disappointed in himself.

***

With the tournament's conclusion, Ezekiel sat alone in an underground room below the arena. Large, empty, dark in colour, and with only stone mounds for furniture, it was a confinement devoid of any intrigue or entertainment. Perfect for Ezekiel to ponder in.

The eldest Zhakkari thought about his younger siblings. Despite how badly that dinner had ended, he thought back on it fondly. His heart swelled with pride when he thought about his younger siblings and their achievements. Though he would never say this, not to them or anyone.

He adored Grace and how she strived for more influence within the Arisclan Bello lands and brought gold back to Zhakkari land. He was as proud as a father when he heard of Samuel's new position on the Kingsclan Council. He could not have felt happier for Promise, her husband, her child, and their new land. He loved that his siblings were living successful lives. Ezekiel never cared for traditional success, but a part of him wondered whether he should follow in their footsteps. He knew he could not fight in battles and tournaments for Arisclan Rashid his entire life.

"Ezekiel," a gravelly voice called out, interrupting his thoughts. He looked up with frustration at the disrupting visitor, Ahmed Rashid.

"Shouldn't you be enjoying your thorough victory somewhere?" he asked him.

"I'm enjoying the silence. Well, I was," Ezekiel snarked. Ahmed chortled at the remark, though his eyes shot warning daggers.

"Very funny, boy," Ahmed said. He paced his way into the room, the metal of his sabatons making a satisfying yet ominous clang as he marched over the jagged stone. He sat on a mound next to Ezekiel.

"Do you need something from me?" Ezekiel asked.

"Not necessarily. But I do think there are some things we ought to discuss," Ahmed admitted. "Regarding your battle conduct, that is."

"Do you not like how hard I was hitting your son during the tournament finale?" Ezekiel asked.

"Like I said, you're a very funny boy," Ahmed remarked. "And a very astute one, apparently."

Ezekiel sat up straight, exhaling deeply out of his nose. He narrowed his eyes, waiting for Ahmed to elaborate.

"The brutality that comes with your specific brand of vitality has served us very well in battle thus far, especially against the Saxe-Barbarians," said Ahmed. "But against our own warriors? It's unnecessary. I can't have my soldiers severely hurt or injured. Especially not my son."

Ezekiel's narrowed eyes squinted further in bewildered incredulity. Of all the grievances that Ahmed Rashid of all people could have possibly had with him, being too vital a warrior was not one he thought he would hear.

"You understand what I'm saying, boy?" Ahmed asked.

"Yes. I'll make sure not to beat them as emphatically next time," Ezekiel scorned.

"You won't be getting the chance to, unfortunately," Ahmed told him. "We're releasing you from our ranks. As of tonight, you are no longer a Clan Rashid warrior."

Ezekiel stared at the leader of his former warrior ranks. He waited for a beastly-belly laugh or a crushing punch to the arm, any indicator that he was joking. When no such indicator came, the initial indignation Ezekiel felt doubled.

"Is this a bizarre fucking joke?"

"Eh, watch your mouth, boy."

"I'm the one who should be calling you '*boy*'," Ezekiel spat. "If I weren't fighting for this stupid fucking clan, you and your men would be nothing more than Saxe-Barbarian slaves thrown out to sea! You couldn't even train your son to beat me, you pathetic bastard."

Ahmed stood up with a gradual menace. "You're aware that those are fighting words, aren't you, boy?"

"You've lost your taste for battle long ago, old man. A fight between us would end in a mercy kill on my part," Ezekiel asserted.

Ahmed's face contorted, their positions changing with him in furious disbelief as Ezekiel stared him down with a bold constitution. The Zhakkari braced himself for a flurry of attacks that came with the signature Rashid tirade of fists and blades. What he had not prepared for was the clan leader's jovial laugh returning.

"You caught me, I was jesting," Ahmed admitted. Ezekiel felt a touch of relief as he relaxed his tensed shoulders and fists. "Although I wasn't jesting *entirely*."

"And what exactly does that mean?" Ezekiel asked.

"You are being released from the ranks, but not for the reasons I've said," Ahmed said.

"Why don't you stop the jesting and tell me what I need to know before I tear your fucking throat out?" Ezekiel threatened, his patience long gone.

Ahmed smiled as if the thought filled him with the greatest jubilation.

"Earlier today, I received a recommendation from the Kingsclans. I was told to no longer associate with anyone named Zhakkari," the Rashid clan leader explained. "I fabricated that excuse about your brutality so you could leave with your dignity intact. But I should have known you'd be stubborn."

Ezekiel's frustration grew with his confusion. His only response was an oafish grunt.

"You've not heard? Your siblings have been incredibly unruly. Raping and killing pleasure-maidens. Cutting the arms of Kingsclan defenders and violently escaping detainment. Everything under the sun!" Ahmed laughed in raucous derision. "Your clan has been blacklisted."

Ezekiel could hardly process the information that had just been unloaded onto him. Rape, murder, and royal cuttings were far removed from even the worst antics he knew his siblings would involve themselves in. But he knew the way Ahmed Rashid behaved when he was lying or joking. He could not sense any dishonesty from Rashid, shaking his belief in his Zhakkari bredrin.

"My siblings would never commit crimes, especially not crimes of that nature," Ezekiel said, deciding to fight on behalf of their innocence regardless. "And even if they did, I don't see why that means I have to leave the Rashid army."

"Do you have dirt in your ears, boy? Two of your siblings committed horrible crimes. They're saying it's a shared conspiracy!" Ahmed roared. "As far as the land's concerned, your family is tainted! I, for one, am not ready to deal with the fallout of having a Zhakkari in my ranks!"

"What if I refuse?"

"Refuse what?!"

"Everything," Ezekiel said. "What if I refuse to believe a word out of your mouth or anyone else's? What if I refuse to accept that my family has been tainted? In fact, what if I refuse to even leave your warrior ranks, old man?"

Ahmed gasped with booming laughter. "All you'll be doing is expediting your demise, stupid fucking boy."

"In what way?" Ezekiel questioned, goading.

Ahmed slammed his fists against the jagged walls, pounding the side of his hand bloody. On this command, six of Arisclan Rashid's finest warriors, wielding daggers and spears, poured into the room. These were the Hustan defenders, tournament fighters, and brave soldiers Ezekiel had shared a battlefield with many times before.

"You could have left this arena and maybe taken a chance. You might have avoided detainment despite your clan being blacklisted!" Ahmed explained, frustrated as ever. "But now, we'll have to chain you up and leave you to rot down here ourselves!"

Ahmed stepped back as the Rashid warriors stepped forward. Ezekiel's eyes flared with intense, unrefined fury and anxious excitement.

"Go on. Fucking try," he goaded as his once quiet room thronged with blades turned against him.

***

Grace lay beside Samuel. The pair of siblings rested under the large V-shaped leaves of a dying tropical tree, their shelter from the night's cold.

Hours had passed since their escape, and feelings of destitution were beginning to set in, especially for Grace. The oldest female Zhakkari's eyes were contemplative.

"So, you didn't rape her, but you *did* murder her?" she asked her brother.

"She tried to murder me. My instincts took over," Samuel confirmed. "I don't think self-defence is a crime worthy of exile. Do you?"

"No."

"Then why do you doubt me?"

Grace rolled her tongue against the roof of her mouth as she thought. This sole movement was enough to have her feel drained of energy.

"I still can't wrap my head around why the Kingsclans would wish to destroy you and sully our family name in the process," Grace sighed. The sight of Jacqueline's smug face as the defenders dragged her out of the gala was singed in her memory.

"I'm sure it has something to do with my first meeting on the council. They disliked my talking points," Samuel explained. "They even compared me to Clan Godwin."

"They disliked your talking points to the extent that they were willing to falsely brand you as a malicious savage and accuse me of conspiring with you?" Grace said, more than baffled by the premise.

Samuel's lips tightened as he pondered many thoughts in quick succession. He found himself overwhelmed as he combed through his mind. None of his thoughts and theories were clear enough to give him the answers they needed. He assessed it was time for action instead.

"If they were willing to detain you, they'll attempt to detain Ezekiel and Promise, too. We need to find them first," Samuel said.

"Ezekiel is attending a Clan Rashid Tournament tonight. I don't think we'll be able to reach him without being caught," Grace said.

"But Promise should be on her new land with her husband. We can reach her," Samuel responded.

"There's a good chance she's already been detained," Grace said. "And even if she hasn't, there's an even greater chance we'll be caught before we can get to her land."

Samuel accepted this possibility with an exasperated grunt. "We must at least try."

***

Ezekiel slammed another warrior's head into the wall, bludgeoning it against a jutted-out rock and driving the blade of a broken-off spear inside for good measure. He growled with a feral fever, his face drenched in Arisclan soldier blood as he stood by a pile of four bodies. The

70

majority of the warriors sent to capture him had their weapons turned against them and their lives ended. With one half of a broken spear in one hand, a dagger in the other, and a hundred bleeding cuts on his body, Ezekiel was more than willing to add a million more if it meant he could fight his way out of detainment. With their clan leader no longer in the vicinity, the remaining two warriors were reluctant to face their rank's former best soldier in war, else they would end up like their comrades. However, giving in was not a viable option.

One of these last two warriors stabbed their spear at Ezekiel with exacting speed. The oldest Zhakkari sibling escaped a blade through the skull by the nearest margin with a shift of his body. Snarling with excitement, Ezekiel stomped forward, meeting the man with a briefly incapacitating knee to the groin. The other warrior swiped at Ezekiel with his spear, cutting a shallow scrape across his body. Ezekiel quickly stepped back before it could have left a deeper cut. He absorbed the pain with a smile on his face and launched his blade at the man, aiming for his neck. The soldier dipped underneath this strike, but that proved to be a mistake. In the time it took him to duck down, Ezekiel closed the distance between the two of them and sank the half-spear into his exposed stomach area.

The man he had struck in the groin rose to his feet, ready for an attack. Ezekiel sent him back where he came from with another strike to the groin, this time with one of his dead comrades' blades. Before he could succumb to the humiliating misery, Ezekiel tackled him. He plunged the knife into one eye and dragged it across the man's face until it met the other socket. This warrior's final moments were spent twitching in debilitating, blind agony. He died of shock soon after.

71

With all six warriors disposed of, Ezekiel searched the room for Ahmed Rashid. He could not see him anywhere within the confines of those blood-painted walls.

Ezekiel rushed out of the room and into a moist, wet hall, dark and dimly lit. He panted with excitement in the manner of a wild animal hunting its prey. Prey that he found in no time at all.

Ahmed Rashid was in the process of fleeing the underground section of the arena. He was about to abscond to an abutting tunnel.

He paused for a moment to scorn Ezekiel. "You're disgustingly stubborn."

Ezekiel pointed the half-broken spear at Ahmed, approaching him with a malicious smile.

"If you're still planning on chaining me, the only way you will is if it's with my dead body," Ezekiel laughed. Ahmed smiled, seeming to welcome the threat.

Ezekiel felt a sudden, sickening crack at the back of his head. He immediately felt weak, his body buckling at the knees. The momentum of energy from his constant killings drained from him, leaving the warrior with no adrenaline and an acute realisation of all the damage that had been inflicted on him.

Ezekiel mustered one last morsel of power to turn around. He wished to see who delivered the defeating blow.

Ibrahim laughed at him from above. He held the mace from the tournament in his hand, its head subtly stained with blood from the Zhakkari's head.

"Don't get upset," Ibrahim mocked.
He clubbed Ezekiel with the mace once more, breaking his nose to add injury to insult.

Ezekiel murmured incomprehensible grumbles in response as his consciousness slipped away from him. Ibrahim and his father mocked him all the while.

A DREADFUL VISIT

PROMISE Zhakkari and Francis Irie enjoyed a night alone on their new land. The couple sat in a chariot's carriage by a freshwater pond that was circled with stones engulfed in dull blue flames for scenic lighting. They looked to the stars, the low roars of their resting lions adding to the calming aura that perfected their special night together.

"I love this part of the land, it's so peaceful and wholesome," Promise said with a child-like innocence.

Francis hugged her tighter, pressing her forehead against his cheek.

"That's why I reserved it for you. To celebrate our marriage," Francis said. "If I could, I would've also reserved the stars."

"Thank you, my love," Promise gushed with joy.
She posited that not much could be done that could sully this moment. One could say the universe took this as a challenge, with the events that followed.

"Promise!" a pair of voices screamed at her from over the horizon. Promise shook as she looked down from the stars and across the pond. She saw two figures sprint around the pond's edge and approach her and her husband. "Promise!" they shouted.

"Do you know those people?" Francis asked, his eyes squinting as the figures hurried towards them.

Promise did not answer him, unsure of whether she did or not. The closer they came towards them, the surer she was that she did.

"Promise, we need to leave! You're in danger! Our family is in danger!" Grace exclaimed as she and Samuel paused their sprint in front of the couple.

Promise had never seen her older siblings so dishevelled. At that moment, they looked like peasants from the poorest lands. The fabric of their clothes was torn to pieces, hanging off them. Bleeding scabs were dispersed across their bodies.

"What's happened to you?!" Promise asked. She stepped out of the carriage, Francis reluctantly following her lead.

"We'll explain it to you in greater detail once we've escaped to safety," Samuel said, catching his breath. "All you need to know is that our family is under attack and you're at risk of being detained."

Promise's face squirmed with terrified concern. Francis felt less worried and more displeased.

"I don't understand. What kind of trouble are the pair of you in?" Francis asked his wife's siblings.

"Our family name has been marred by false accusations of murder, treason, and much more," Grace said. "They tried to unjustly imprison us. They'll try the same with you and Ezekiel."

"Are you being serious?" Promise asked, her fretful eyes quivering.

"Why would they want to detain you for crimes you did not commit?" Francis questioned.

"All of this can be explained in depth soon, very soon. But at this moment in time, our main priority should be leaving this land," Samuel insisted with frustration.

"Where's your baby boy?" Grace asked Promise.

"Joseph's being taken care of at Francis' sister Sali's home," Promise said. Francis gave a stiff confirming nod.

"Good, he's safe there. We ought to go somewhere where *we'll* be safe," Samuel said.

"Halt, Zhakkari filth!" a shaky voice shouted, interrupting their conversation. "Stop right there!"

Legions of Kingsclan defenders on tiger-drawn chariots were riding over the horizon and around the pond.

"We must leave at once!" Samuel demanded.
He leapt into the chariot that Promise and Francis had just left. Grace quickly followed.

"Let's go, Francis!" Promise urged her husband as she stepped in with reluctance.

"I can't make sense of any of this!" Francis complained. He looked between them and the Kingsclan defenders as if to try and figure out the situation for himself first.

"I trust they'll explain it to us later. Enter the chariot, dear," Promise urged. Francis refused, glaring at Samuel and Grace with distrust as the Kingsclan defenders prepared their seizure attack in the background.

"Rain hell-fire!" the head of the Kingsclan legion ordered his archers.

They halted their tigers from across the pond. The archers coated the blades of their arrows with the blue flames of the surrounding pond stones before placing them in their bows and letting loose. The flaming arrows flew over the pond and descended over their position.

Samuel narrowly avoided being skewered as he ducked. Instinctively, Grace grabbed her sister and pulled her downwards to safety as they crouched behind the chariot walls. An arrow skimmed past Grace's arm as she protected Promise, burning her shoulder and leaving a thin cut. The siblings braced for impact as dozens of arrows flew past and around them. They faced the bottom of the carriage they hid in, the whirring sounds of the flame-engulfed projectiles crashing against the chariot's metal.

Once the arrow-fire ceased, they raised their heads. Grace attended to the scorched bruise on her arm as Samuel fumbled at the reins of the chariot in a panic.

Promise peered over her cover behind the inside of the chariot to see if her husband had been as lucky as they were in avoiding the fire. All she saw was that he was no longer standing. Francis Irie's body lay on the floor, burnt and punctured with the three arrows that had struck him through his liver, abdomen, and brain.

"Francis?" Promise called out to her lifeless husband. She waited for his response, denying the harsh reality she saw before her.

"Burn that Zhakkari carriage down! *Now*!" the lead defender of their Kingsclan attackers ordered as his archers prepared more fire arrows.

Promise was not allowed the time to acknowledge her husband's demise. Their chariot raced forward, the lions galloping as Samuel whipped their reins with urgency.

"Francis?!" Promise uttered with an outstretched hand as they left his corpse far behind them.

***

With aching arms, Samuel rode the chariot nonstop until they found themselves out of range in a marshy grassland away from Civcaz proper.

After a night of constant riding, he was finally sure they were out of any Kingsclan's clutches.

"They've given up the chase," Samuel sighed with relief as he released the reins. His palms were rough and red from having held them too tightly for too long.

"Thank the virtues," Grace gasped. Without another word, both she and Samuel checked on Promise.

The last-born Zhakkari had spent the journey in silence. Their youngest sister sat in the chariot in frozen discomfort, unblinking and unmoving but for light shivers of shock and cold. The two older siblings shared a demoralised glance, both non-verbally asking, "What should we do?"

Grace rested a loving arm over her younger sister's shoulder. "Promise, we're sorry," she said with awkward condolences. "What happened to Francis…it was a very unfortunate conseq-"

"You killed him," Promise whimpered, her voice as delicate as a baby's. "You killed the father of my child."

"The Kingsclan's killed your husband. They would have attacked you whether we came or not," Samuel said.

"All the same," Promise sighed with sorrow.
She wriggled her way out of Grace's embrace and sank deeper into her seat, too tired and broken to do anything but lie there with her eyes closed. A quiet streaming tear fell from each of her shut eyelids and dampened the river emblem on her Clan Irie necklace.

Samuel and Grace decided to leave her alone for the time being. The sibling duo wore regretful countenances.

**

Days later, the Zhakkari siblings were settling into their unofficial exile. They stumbled upon an old stone house with mud floors and holes in the brick wall, using it as their base of shelter. They survived on flame-roasted meat from

78

the bodies of dead animals they found in empty fields, trips to collect water from a river in an abandoned town, and hope. Hope soon became the scarcest resource on that list.

Samuel sat in the corner of their claustrophobic abode, his face stained with particles of mud as he read a withered piece of brown paper. Grace sat in the middle next to Promise, who slept on a frayed cloth. In the days they had spent there in hiding, this seemed to be all their little sister was able to do. Her siblings could count the number of hours she was strong enough to stay awake each day on only one hand.

Grace caressed Promise's darling face. "We could not find ourselves in a worse situation if we tried."

"You're right, sister," Samuel said as he stood up from his corner. "Which means the only option is to do all in our power to make it better."

He dumped the weathered page he had been reading on the floor in front of her. "I found this whilst fetching water in the remains of a village."

Grace's eyes scanned the paper. It was a news update from the morning after they had escaped the Kingsclan men.

"*Ezekiel, the eldest child of the infamous Commonsclan Zhakkari, was detained by Arisclan Rashid forces. The manhunt to detain his illicit siblings who evaded justice the previous night is ongoing*," Grace read aloud.

Samuel bowed his head in acknowledgement of the *good* news. Grace was not impressed.

"I already assumed this was the case. How does reading this help us?" she complained.

"Confirmation of what we assumed to be true is good. Now we know for certain that Ezekiel is still alive, meaning we can plan on freeing him," Samuel suggested. "And once we're together again, we can figure out how to rectify the land's mistake in persecuting our family."

"The next step is risking fate to free him? You've settled on that plan?"

"I have."

"Why? Has hunger made you go mad?" Grace scoffed.

"Again, what other choice do we have? What else can we do but try?" Samuel said.

Grace was unable to refute his logic. In a way, such a ridiculous plan filled her with hope. Whilst she had found herself lacking in energy due to their circumstances, Samuel, whom she had often mocked for being a spiritual coward, was seemingly possessed by an impulsive courage.

Grace determined they could use his dumbstruck bravery well. It was the only way they could cope with how far they had fallen and work on climbing back to their rightful places.

A PLAN EXECUTED

GRACE Zhakkari could not believe what her brother was proposing. "Out of every plan, you chose that one?"

"It's what we can do considering the limited resources we have at our disposal," Samuel said with a shrug.

"I see," Grace accepted.

Samuel always had a unique talent for formulating unorthodox schemes that were often too ingenious to fail but too strange to have any practical execution.

"You still know how to tame wild lion cubs. Correct?" Samuel asked.

Grace nodded with pride. It was one of the many miscellaneous skills she mastered as a child that the other siblings had not bothered with. The only reason *she* bothered to was for another showing of her competitive superiority, to do something the others could not. She never knew this would be useful.

"Good, now all I need to do is reconnect with someone who can help us execute the plan using a cub," Samuel said.

"You know someone who lives out here?" Grace asked, surprised. In the days they spent in this grassy wasteland, she saw no more than twelve people, with her siblings being two of them.

"Yes. I believe there is one man we can rely on if we can find him," Samuel said. "I'll look for him now. It'll probably take me a while, so you needn't worry even if you don't see me for a few days."

"You'd better be careful out there," Grace warned him.

"Make sure to look after Promise whilst I'm gone," Samuel said as he gestured to her.

Grace glanced at her sleeping sister. That morning, Promise woke with tears streaming down her face, only to fall back into a deep sleep. Grace rested a hand over hers.

"You don't have to remind me to look after my baby sister," she said as Samuel left. He rolled his eyes at her with a smile, then exited the half-corroded stone structure.

***

Like a lowly rat, Ezekiel writhed across the floors of his cell. Iron bars, marching defenders, and a revoltingly moist sedimentary rock corridor of leaking sewage water were all that stood between him and his freedom. A ladder was attached to a wall that led to a hole that would take him above ground. He caught a glimpse of the blue sky above from the corner of his confinement. Freedom seemed close enough to imagine striving for, yet too far to try for.

Ezekiel watched as someone climbed down the hole and into the dungeon halls. With pomp and swagger, they walked past the defenders, the bottom of their sabatons squelching from the moist stones below.

Ezekiel's eyes tracked Ibrahim with hate as he stopped in front of his cell. He gripped the metal bars as his former friend smirked smugly.

"Are you enjoying your stay?" Ibrahim mocked.

"I am. Why don't you come inside for a visit?" Ezekiel retorted as he stood up to confront him. Had the cell bars not been in between them, he would have taken both of Ibrahim's beautiful eyes out.

"You didn't have to end up here," Ibrahim sighed.

"What was my alternative path?" Ezekiel spat back at him. "Leaving the ranks with my tail between my legs and being detained by the Kingsclans anyway?"

Ibrahim shook his head like a lordly father scolding his unruly son. "You don't have to fight everything, Ezekiel. Sometimes you ought to just do what you're told."

"Like you're one to do?" Ezekiel asked with derision.

"My father wants you rotting down here, my clan wants you rotting down here, and the lands want you rotting down here. Who am I to act against all that?" Ibrahim questioned. "And with how sour you're being, I'm starting to like you rotting down here."

Ezekiel spat on Ibrahim's armour. Ibrahim laughed nonchalantly as he pushed himself away from the cell bars.

Ezekiel watched the eldest Rashid son swagger down the hall and up the ladder to the surface. He had grown to hate the flippant attitude he once found amusing.

"Spineless fucker," Ezekiel grunted.

***

Night fell. The cold winds from outdoors drafted heavily into the holes in the wall of their depleted shelter. Grace shivered in the corner of the minuscule house, still waiting for Samuel's return.

Grace had spent the majority of that day with no company. She finally had someone to talk to again once Promise awoke from her day of deep, depressed slumbers.

Promise's bloodshot eyes surveyed the room before landing on Grace. "This is our life," she bemoaned.

"It won't be for long," Grace assured her.

Promise sighed. "Francis," she mourned under her breath. "Why would they do that to my sweet Francis?"

Grace's head hung heavy with guilt as she watched her sister shiver with misery.

Shortly after, Samuel made his return. He brought company. A wiry man with a sturdy jaw and guileful eyes followed him into the house with a bemused expression.

"This is where my clan leaders sleep? How the virtuous have fallen," the wiry man quipped. Grace had already decided that she disliked him.

"This is Oliver Bala. A former member of our clan and a friend of mine who chose to live freely out here as opposed to the villages years ago," Samuel introduced.

"Nice to meet you, my ladies," Oliver said, bowing to Grace and Promise. Grace greeted Oliver with a nod. Promise ignored him.

"*He's* helping us execute our lion-cub plan to free Ezekiel?" Grace asked.

"Don't sound so disappointed, Madame Zhakkari. I am *very* competent when it comes to the arts of hiding and sneaking," he laughed. Neither sister was amused.

"I'm surprised you found someone willing to help us," Promise commented.

"Samuel and I share a fond history. He's the one who introduced me to my wife," Oliver explained.

"Who he's still with to this day," Samuel added, mirroring Bala's smile with pride.

Oliver's smile dropped. "No, actually. I forgot to tell you that she left me," he corrected.

Samuel's smile evaporated, too. "What? Why?"

"When I found out the twins we raised were the product of another man's seed, I exploded in anger, to say the least,"

84

Oliver explained. "She didn't even apologise. She just packed her belongings and left me for the very same man."

Promise was appalled. "That's horrible. How could a woman even think of doing such a thing?" she gasped in innocent disbelief.

"That's Civcaz folk for you. No care for honour anymore. None at all," Oliver sighed.

Samuel shook his head in solidarity. "It was disillusionment with Civcaz as a whole that made him and his family move here in the first place," he explained to his sisters. "It's also why he's so willing to help us."

"I have to. Especially with what I heard they're planning to do with your land," Oliver said.

"What have you heard?" Grace asked.

"That they plan on revoking your status as a Commonsclan and scorching your fields," he explained. "They're rationalising it as *stopping another Clan Godwin before it's too late.*"

"Naturally," Samuel sighed. He ground his teeth as flashbacks of William Khoza and Christian Osei berating him at the Kingsclan Council meeting ran through his head.

"Cheer up. My help is the first step in ensuring that doesn't happen," Oliver said.

"Mhm," Samuel agreed. "Now all we need is to steal a lion cub for Grace to tame. Then we can move forward."

Grace thought about their scheme as she stared at the ground. Though she would not voice it, she had little faith in their abilities to free Ezekiel or fix their countless other problems. But it was at least a better plan than having no plan, she conceded.

***

Ezekiel sat up in his cell as midnight came to pass. The Zhakkari warrior was the very image of strained endurance.

His skin had become rough and dry from the accumulation of unwashed dirt and sweat during his capture. His stomach constricted like a snake eating its tail. He took in heavy breaths to dispel the pain that came with no food and a cupful of water. With his shivers and clicking jaw, he put his mind away from his painful hunger, occupying it with thoughts of his dear siblings.

Whether or not they committed the crimes they were being accused of was of little concern. Whether they were captives or exiles, Ezekiel planned on seeing them again and killing anyone who tried to stop him. But as his body weakened with every severe hour spent within these walls, it seemed he would never see sunlight.

As he stared onwards, Ezekiel felt a disturbance. He was not alone. The defenders guarding the halls of the dungeon stumbled as the underground space shook.

The floor beneath Ezekiel rumbled and quaked, its sharp-edged rock surface scraping at his skin as he stood up to find out what was going on. He could hear the origin of the rumblings. It was not coming from underneath but from above. Something was rocking the earth above them and reverberating with enough force to tremble these underground quarters.

"What in all souls is going on up there?" complained one of the defenders, thrusting his spear to the ceiling in anger. As if to challenge him, the tremors doubled in sound and vibration.

The defender closest to the ladder sighed lazily as his comrades in the corridor urged him to check.

A guard from above ground fell down the hole, knocking the man off the ladder as they both crashed with a loud, wet thud. The man who had been climbing the ladder was prepared to curse out the faller until he saw there was no faller to curse out. The body that had collapsed into the hall was dead, with claw marks littering it and the head severed from its neck.

"Soldiers, help! Help!" screamed the panicked voice of one of the defenders above ground. The shaking tremors were peppered with accompanying noises of shrieks, growls, and tearing flesh.

Ezekiel watched every single one of the dozen roaming defenders leave their posts in the underground dungeon halls, rushing one after another up the ladder to help with whatever gruesome situation was being dealt with above ground. He walked to the edge of his cell, his hands wrapped tightly around the iron bars as he listened carefully.

There was silence at first. Then, carnage.

The screams grew louder and more painful. The earth shook more violently. He could smell the stale metallicity of countless suffering men. Ezekiel tried to imagine what could be causing the carnage. Perhaps they had fallen victim to a surprise Saxe-Barbarian attack? But that could not be the case. He did not hear the cheers of wily men of the sea, only deep growls of a beast.

Blood leaked down the dungeon hole as a Rashid man crawled down the ladder in a panic. One of his arms had been chewed to the elbow, and three-quarters of his face was made into a pulpy mess. The blood alone made his skin red as opposed to Civcaz-brown.

If Ezekiel knew the man before, he still would not be able to recognise him at a glance. With fear in his one half-carved-out good eye, he backed away from the ladder, looking at the hole upwards. Visibly weak and only set to grow worse, the man stumbled forward, whimpering as he clutched his missing hand with his injured other. He swayed from side to side in a daze and fell towards Ezekiel's cell.

"Save…me," the man croaked as his one hand slid down the bars, wetting them with thick blood.

The man slid down the other side of his cell, slowly succumbing to death. Ezekiel grimaced at the painful showing but took no time to mourn. He used the blood on the cell bars as a lubricant as he stretched his hand out.

Ezekiel rifled through every compartment of the dead man's armour. He found no keys but recovered a small dagger and a miniature blade.

He walked to the end of his cell and reached his hand around the outside. The imprisoned Zhakkari used both small weapons to pick the lock.

***

Much later, Ezekiel climbed out of the hole, having escaped the dungeon. A barren field of grass that was crushed and tempered until it was hard as concrete awaited him, hosting decorations of the nastiest order.

If he set out to count the number of dead Arisclan defenders in the area, midnight would have become dawn before he finished counting. The pungent smell of the rotting corpses assaulted his nostrils. The sight placed a touch of fear in Ezekiel's heart. Not because of the sheer number of deceased warriors that had been left there, but because he could not see what had caused this massacre.

As Ezekiel traversed the field of death, he finally saw it, resting at the bottom of the other side of the hill in all its terrible glory. The grandest lion that Ezekiel had ever laid his eyes on rested on blood-soaked grasses below.

He guessed the beast was at least twelve feet in length and would not be surprised if it reached a thousand pounds in weight. The monstrous lioness was covered in blood and blade injuries. She chewed on the body of a half-dead warrior, a meal she picked out from a pile of them next to her. Beside her was a much smaller lion cub. Strangely, the baby creature was completely drenched in blood, but of a slightly different colour and consistency than the blood on the fields and the mother's jaw.

Ezekiel gulped with a fear he had never before experienced as he slowly traced his way back up the hill. His heart pounded with brutal force as he took special care not to make a single sound. He had never seen such a wild beast on civilised Civcaz land unless brought there intentionally, even in a place like the dungeon-hole fields.

He thanked the creature in his mind for having allowed his escape to be possible.

***

Ezekiel bolted down a sandy shore with nothing but the moonlight to guide his way as he sought the open water. Since he had crept away from the lioness and snuck over the fields, he wondered where he was to run to. He wondered where he was to find his siblings, and how he would join them without being caught by the Kingsclans. The stars of fate aligned perfectly for him when he reached the water. He found his siblings sitting in a large rowboat.

"My virtues. He's out already?" Promise said. She saw him barrelling towards them with passionate excitement.

"The lioness must have eviscerated every single defender. I would've liked to see that scene," Samuel said with simultaneous delight and disgust. Promise crossed her arms as Grace stared on.

"This is how fugitives spend their time?" Ezekiel asked as he jumped into the rowboat beside his brother and sisters.

"You saved us a lot of time. We were just about to come free you from your cell," Samuel said. "How'd you break out so quickly?"

"A defender dropped dead in front of my cell, so I was able to escape using a blade I took from him. By the time I freed myself and climbed up the hole to the fields, every defender on patrol was already dead," Ezekiel explained. "Speaking of which, we'd be wise to leave here immediately. There's a gargantuan fucking lion on the loose," he added.

"We're aware," said Grace, sounding responsibly guilty. Ezekiel's eyes lit with realisation. He recalled the useless lion-cub taming training that Grace would brag about in their youth. He figured out why the lion cub was covered in different-coloured blood. He realised that Grace must have tamed and stolen it away from its mother whilst she was sleeping. Then they must have lathered it in the blood and meat of other animals to enhance its stench so the mother would be able to track it. Then someone must have sneaked in and placed it in the fields, using it to lure the lioness towards the overground dungeon.

He was not sure how they accomplished that last part without getting caught back on Civcaz land, but was impressed that they did. Appreciative of his sibling's ingenuity, a wicked smile crept onto his face.

"It's great to see you," Ezekiel laughed with relief as he picked up a rowing oar. Together, he and Grace took them away from Civcaz shores and out to sea.

"Now that we're all back together again, we can start thinking of actual plans to solve our dilemma," Samuel said as they rowed away.

Ezekiel laughed with anger and amusement. "What's there to think about?" he scoffed. "We're going to fucking war over this."

A LAND DIVIDED

PROMISE Zhakkari hated to see her brothers and sister argue. Even when they were united by the shared experience of being despised by their land, witch-hunted by its people, and at risk of having even more stripped away from them, the Zhakkaris struggled to stay on the same page.

"I never took my siblings for baseless cowards," Ezekiel insulted. Ever since he was brought back to the deconstructed stone abode the Zhakkaris had been hiding in since their unofficial exile, he refused to sit down or even rest his body by the walls. He acted as if doing so was symbolically accepting their current fate.

"There's a difference between cowardice and being reasonably wary!" Samuel insisted. "I think you can forgive me for not wanting to throw ourselves into a war, considering our current awful position!"

"They took our land, turned all clans against us, and imprisoned us without just cause!" Ezekiel shouted. "We should destroy the Kingsclans and then the Arisclans. What reason do we have not to?"

"We'll lose. Horribly," Grace said.

"What kind of pathetic prediction is that?" Ezekiel scoffed at her.

"It's a rational one, though I'd hardly expect you, of all people, to understand. Rationality was never your strong suit," Grace scoffed. "Even with all of Clan Zhakkari's resources at our disposal, we'd lose a war against the Kingsclan armies. That shouldn't need explaining. What chance do we stand now that we have nothing?"

"None of that *shit* concerns me. They've disrespected and diminished us. The only worthwhile response is bloodshed of the highest order," Ezekiel asserted. "We should gather up men for battle, storm their Hustans, and show we're not a clan that can be so easily destroyed."

Grace raised an eyebrow at him in the same manner one would when unsure of how to respond to a petulant child coming up with ridiculous ideas.

"There is a middle ground here," Samuel said. "We shouldn't start a war just yet. We *should* gather up the men and women of our clan. I want to see how many people will support getting this witch-hunt against us overturned."

Ezekiel and Grace pondered over the proposition for a short while. Neither was particularly enthusiastic in their support of the idea, though neither could disagree.

"That could work, I suppose," Grace accepted.

"Right," Ezekiel grunted. "It all ends the same way anyway."

Samuel turned to Promise, who had been silently listening to their argument whilst braiding her hair.

"What do you think? Should we gather our people?" Samuel asked her.

She nodded in agreement. She was too tired to have argued back, even if she *did* have any disagreements.

Promise would have said or done anything to put an end to the sibling fights. She did not care what they did next.

All she wanted to do was see her baby. Or at the very least, mourn her Francis in peace.

***

Oliver Bala travelled to Civcaz proper in the most disorganised chariot one could have. He carried dozens of chickens and hundreds of eggs in between bales of straw in a back carriage that was drawn forward by a leopard with dirt caked into its fur. Unbeknownst to the few defenders who had haphazardly checked his wares on the rough path, the Zhakkari siblings lay cooped up underneath. Ezekiel, Grace, Samuel, and Promise were hidden by clumps of straw, broken shells, and egg yolk.

While her siblings twitched and twisted, writhing subtly from the deep discomfort of being packed together for such a long journey, Promise slept well. Since her husband's death, sleep occupied the majority of her time. It came to the point that, despite her grief, her siblings would chastise her for it. But she did not care. The events in her dreams were much sweeter than anything real life had to offer. Memories of simpler times.

The memory that stood out to her with the greatest fondness was her wedding day. Hundreds of Commonsclan Zhakkari men and women mingled on Arisclan Irie soil to celebrate the marriage that would join their families in spirit. She remembered the mess of butterflies that was her stomach and how much she enjoyed the sensation. She remembered how handsome and noble Francis looked and how lovingly he smiled down at her. But the one aspect of the wedding that was emphasised to her through these dreams of memories was how out of character her siblings had been that day. Their out-of-character behaviour was positive, nonetheless.

Their intense rivalries and urges to constantly bicker were set aside on that wedding day. Samuel and Grace were not engaged in even the slightest form of aggressive competition for once, both focused on keeping the peace as they danced and sang in joy with the other guests. Ezekiel also mellowed out that day. She remembered watching in delight as he dropped his demeanour of a brutal warmonger and took up the joviality of a proud older brother with laughs galore.

Promise's siblings were never happier than on the day of her wedding. Subsequently, she had never felt happier herself. It was perfect. She could not recall anything that she had ever wanted more in her childhood than the festivities of that day and what they represented. She cursed herself for the naive belief she had at the time about it lasting.

Promise never realised how easily it could all be taken away from her. In the present day, her husband was dead, her baby was miles away from her, and her brothers and sisters were barely holding it together in times of agonising hardship. What else could she do to escape from it all other than sleep?

***

Promise woke up to an unholy amalgamation of furious screams, cackling laughter, and the rowdy shouts of frustrated people. She saw she had been left on a blanket at the back of an old barn with dried animal blood stains decorating the walls.

Her siblings and Oliver Bala were in front of her. Ezekiel, Grace, and Samuel stood on a stage made from the roofless back carriage of Bala's chariot and the stacked hay within it. In front of them was the rowdy, insolent crowd of vehement Clan Zhakkari villagers. They had managed to begrudgingly gather their people whilst she slumbered. Their people, for the most part, were treating such an event with negativity ranging from feeling very hesitant to utterly incandescent at being brought there.

"You've disgraced your family and your clan!" shouted a man in the crowd, spitting directly at Samuel.

"I've done no such thing! As I've explained, I was forced to kill out of self-defence, and all the other accusations were completely false!" Samuel explained to the belligerent crowd, becoming incandescent himself.

"And we're to believe that without question?" a woman in the crowd shouted in defiance.

"We believe him," Grace said, Ezekiel raising his head in corroboration. "No brother of ours would ever commit such heinous acts, especially not whilst serving on the Kingsclan Council!"

"How are we to know that this isn't irrational sibling loyalty?!" another woman called them out.

"They say you aided him!" the man beside her added.

"All false assertions with zero proof," Grace said with a soft yet bold certainty in her voice. "Surely you're not inclined to believe tall tales blindly?"

The people of their clan muttered to each other as they considered the extent to which they did. Some concluded that perhaps they did not, their belligerence lessening. Others were not convinced, scowling at the siblings and projecting their shame onto them.

Ezekiel stepped to the end of the hay stage in front of his younger siblings. His eyes burned with indignation. The crowd quietened down as his eyes scorched across them with harsh judgement.

"The scrutiny from other clans has caused you to forget that we are the leaders of your land. You must remain loyal, even when you feel like you shouldn't be," Ezekiel said. "If the Kingsclans succeed in completely fucking us, they'll destroy our land, which includes your homes. Failure to stand by us will have you struggling to put roofs over your head and food in your children's fucking bellies."

Ezekiel's harsh premonitions had a somewhat persuasive quality to them. A majority of the belligerent crowd, even those who had been screaming the loudest accusations, were gradually becoming convinced of their need to support the siblings. On the other hand, a select few were encouraged to challenge him back.

"That's our only choice? We are to bow down to our clan overlords and do as they say in spite of their potential guilt?" asked a man in the crowd with sardonic contempt.

"You heard them! Once we're officially destroyed as a clan, our lands will be scorched!" another man argued in defence of the Zhakkaris. "Do you think the other clans are going to let us live on their land after our homes are taken away?" he asked.

"I'd rather have my home destroyed than be in support of horrific siblings abusing their powers to get away with crimes against Civcaz!" said a woman from the select few in great defiance to the siblings. Her passionate cries built up the raucous bouts between the crowd as the people of Clan Zhakkari fought amongst each other over whether to support the siblings or condemn them to hell.

Samuel, Grace, and Ezekiel shouted and bargained in attempts to calm the crowd down. All efforts proved useless as the shouts and cries grew more potent and forceful.

Promise's head and body ached from all the noise and commotion. She could no longer rest and pretend none of it was happening. She had to intervene.

"Silence!" Promise screamed with a pleading passion. With her blanket wrapped over her shoulders, she stepped onto the hay stage, pushing past all of her siblings to bring herself in front of the crowd. She wanted to give a speech.

"I understand your hesitance to support us. You have no way of knowing for sure that we're telling the truth. But we ask you to have faith in your clan leaders. Not out of an enforcement of your loyalties but out of the virtue of your souls!" the youngest Zhakkari shouted.

Tears streamed down Promise's face. Her voice cracked with pain. The crowds settled to listen once more to a Zhakkari sibling on stage. This time, with less disturbed disinclination.

"The people who accuse us of many wrongdoings are lacking in all four of the virtues, and I don't say that out of a petulant need to diminish and insult. I say it out of regretful sorrow!" Promise cried out. "In their efforts to detain us at any cost, they killed an innocent man with negligent cruelty! My husband, Francis of the Arisclan Irie family, was carelessly shot with arrows directed at us! We now mourn his death because of the actions of the Kingsclan Council!"

Promise's older siblings watched her in awe. The crowds were captivated by sympathy and disbelief. Their murmurs were welcomed this time as Promise allowed the information she had just provided to simmer. After a moment, she cleared her throat to speak once more.

"What has been done to our family is nothing short of an egregious miscarriage of justice! A serving of suffering force-fed to those who did *nothing* wrong!" Promise shrieked. "My dear Francis was killed! I haven't seen my son in so long! My family has been torn, and if you let them defunct our clan and destroy our land, yours will tear also!"

A shift occurred in the room. One that her older siblings were surprised could have been created by her. Promise had not completely convinced those of Clan Zhakkari to back them wholeheartedly, but she had at least dampened out the dissension and curried more favour.

Enough favour to have the people consider acting in their support.

A STAND TAKEN

SAMUEL Zhakkari slept in fear the night prior. Fear that he would be snatched during his slumber and forced to answer to the Kingsclan Councils.

The Zhakkari siblings were taking a substantial risk in trusting that no member of their clan would report their presence back in Civcaz before the time was right. The siblings agreed it was a test of loyalty. If they could not trust their people to keep quiet for a single night, they could not trust them to stand by them in the face of injustice.

The Zhakkari siblings also agreed to stay in hiding near the carriage in the barn until the grandstand they had planned. That way, if a member of their clan decided to betray them and inform on their whereabouts to other clans, they would be able to make a hasty escape.

Later, Samuel's curiosity beat out his fear. He decided to explore the land of his people. Their time spent on the run was the longest he had spent away from Zhakkari soil in his life. He wanted to see if anything had changed.

During the short amount of time they were in unofficial exile, substantial changes had been made. The land was of poor quality and struggled to yield as many crops, just as he had last seen, but had still depleted in quality significantly.

He found more people roaming the streets aimlessly in the early mornings, more people frequenting taverns, and more people fighting and stealing. None of these sights were major causes for concern. But such a decline was supposed to take place over a longer period of time, which is what concerned him.

Samuel trekked up a hill with a lake between it and a Zhakkari village. As he reached the summit, one large section caught his eye as the most pertinent example of the area's decline. A family's house that was estranged from the central village houses, surrounded by farmland.

He saw three young boys running around a cornfield, each with a flagon in hand. Clearly drunk, the boys exhibited the crass behaviour typical of their level of inebriation. One had a black eye from which he had not learnt a lesson. He started a fight with another boy, pushing him. The other boy obliged, beating his face in with a flagon until the other eye went black. The third boy was in a completely different world, relieving himself on the corn as he poured drink over the stalk, emptying his bladder and chalice in one disrespectful motion. Had they been teenagers, Samuel might have still been disappointed, yet he would have understood their wasted rebellion. The fact that none of these boys could have been older than twelve is what disgusted him.

At the end of the cornfield, Samuel saw what he assumed to be their father, the head farmer. The man, frail and gormless, sat on a straw chair as if he were already dead. He appeared as weak of spirit as he was of body. He watched his three sons, doing nothing to discipline their behaviour. It was almost as if, despite wanting to in his heart, he was physically and mentally unable.

Samuel grimaced. He thought back to the farmer in the village when he was growing up. When his parents were away, the farmer would look after him and let him sit in the fields to read all day in peace.

A few times, unruly children would run onto the field looking for mischief. A few of the other children who would torment Samuel during their schooling would confront him on the fields to inflict more abuse on him. But Samuel never had to worry about that for long, as the farmer would chase them away. On some occasions, the farmer would take time out of his day to teach them how to behave, making up for the failures of their parents.

The old farmer from Samuel's childhood took great care of both the children and his farmlands. A far cry from what he had observed from the farmer at these cornfields.

***

Hours later, Samuel stood on a field west of the Clan Zhakkari Hustan. Grace was to one side of him, Ezekiel and Promise to the other. The Zhakkari siblings stood together bravely. They were supported by their clan members, who occupied the fields behind them, hundreds of people strong. The people of the lands of Clan Zhakkari stood together in solidarity, preparing for what was soon to come.

Kingsclan warriors marched in a legion even larger than the Zhakkari clan crowd that had gathered. Banners with the emblems of Hustan strongholds and crowns flying on tall flags propped up by spears were waved to the sky, intimidating some of the Zhakkari village folk.

Christian Osei led the Kingsclan legions. He rode a roaring male lion as large as the lioness that massacred Ezekiel's captors. William Khoza rode a smaller leopard

101

beside him. The Khoza clan leader wore a haughty, frustrated scowl on his face, while Osei was of a much calmer and more confident disposition.

With countless bannermen behind them, Kingsclan Osei and Kingsclan Khoza confronted Commonsclan Zhakkari with self-aggrandising flair.

"Ezekiel, Grace, Samuel, and Promise Zhakkari," Christian greeted with a tense smile as he stopped his legion of clan members metres away from theirs. "I'm sure you understand the implications of your being here."

The Zhakkari siblings met him with faces as stern as stone. The people of their land mimicked their expressions, multiple scores of scorn. William Khoza scoffed at them with a pompous turning up of his nose.

"Civilians of Commonsclan Zhakkari. Let it be known that by hosting fugitives of Civcaz, you are of the highest guilt by proxy and may be subjected to the same punishments and fates as they will be," Khoza dictated.

A few members of the Zhakkari Clan were made uneasy by these assertions, but none failed to continue standing their ground in the face of it.

"Members of Kingsclans Osei and Khoza. Let it be known that your leaders detained and attacked my siblings and I on unlawful grounds for crimes we are not guilty of. Thus, we refuse any punishment," Samuel retorted.

"We, the people of Clan Zhakkari, are taking an official grandstand against your rulings," Grace affixed.

Ezekiel and Promise ratified their claims with bowing nods, a gesture that the crowds of their clan copied.

William Khoza winced at their gall. Christian Osei was much more amused.

102

The Kingsclan Osei leader dismounted his lion. He rubbed down his finely-cropped curly hair and adjusted the jewels around his armour as he approached them.

The siblings braced themselves as Osei walked towards them. He made sure to stop only a half-foot away from the four, as if to respect an invisible partition. He greeted them with another one of his signature smiles before speaking.

"I'd like it if we could end this as amicably as possible," Christian said with a charming smirk.

As handsome, cheerful, and warm as he was, Samuel could feel a chilling cold in his presence. He could not shake the feeling that the Kingsclan leader's kind eyes were putting a curse on his soul.

"How amicably?" Promise asked, looking at him, but making sure to avoid direct eye contact.

Christian glanced back at William, then returned to facing the siblings. "We're prepared to willingly let you exile yourselves without recourse to violence," he said. "You'll still be stripped of your status as a Commonsclan, and your people will have to find new lands, but they will not be hurt, and you will no longer be hunted."

The Zhakkari siblings exchanged glances. None were willing to express their true thoughts for the time being.

"How will this end if we don't accept?" Ezekiel asked. Christian Osei laughed. "Let's not allow it to get to that stage. The terms we offered you are-"

"How will this end if we don't accept?" Ezekiel interrupted, repeating himself in a more menacing tone.

Christian's eyes flashed with a brief menace of their own. For a moment, even Ezekiel braced himself for a potential show of brutality.

The Zhakkaris watched Christian's sunnier disposition endure. The Osei leader chuckled as he turned away from them. He made the short walk back to his legion and mounted his lion. Once settled, he looked at them again.

"You have two days to accept your exile and leave Civcaz without any due harm," Christian asserted. "If we find you're still here, our armies will sweep through your lands, interpret you and your people's refusal to cooperate as the treason it is, and exercise our right to kill."

"Very well," Samuel said.

Tension hung thick in the air as the Kingsclan Osei and Khoza forces removed themselves from their land. The uneasiness that had crept into the Zhakkari clan's crowd quietly vibrated through the men and women there in the form of nervous chatter.

Promise sighed, resting a hand over her forehead. "Does this mean we have two days until we have to fight Kingsclan armies?"

"We're not accepting that exile. So it does," Grace said.

"As I said, it was going to end in the same way," Ezekiel grunted.

Samuel sighed in concession to his older brother's point. "We'll have to prepare for battle," he said. "A battle with the potential to explode into full-scale war."

A BRUTAL PREPARATION

GRACE Zhakkari trained for battle in the indoor yard where her parents raised her and her siblings. Any nostalgia present within her heart and mind was clouded by anger. With a bow and arrow prepped, she aimed for a large jackfruit propped on a rock table across the pond from her. She shot several arrows at the target until it was a scattered mess falling off the table. In her mind, it was not just a jackfruit. In her mind, she visualised Jacqueline of Clan Bello's head being obliterated.

Grace still could not fathom what Jacqueline did to her that day at the gala. That lie she told about her and Samuel's 'proclivities' vindicated the Kingsclan defender's decision to humiliate her, dragging her out of the hall for all of Arisclan Bello to see. She tried to put the event out of her mind, but the pain from the ignominy she experienced that night would always resurface in her heart. As did the image of Jacqueline's smug face in her head.

Grace could always tell that Jacqueline was jealous of her. The Bello daughter's bitter envy, contrasting against her Zhakkarian arrogant pride, was an apparent dynamic in the pair's false friendship. Grace avoided bringing attention to this apparent dynamic, although she admitted to herself that she was guilty of subtly provoking Jacqueline, poking fun at her jealousy and watching it grow. Such as singing for her parents or flirting with her brother Michel.

Grace oscillated between two patterns of thought. One being that she ought to have been less haughty and arrogant growing up, that if she had been kinder, perhaps Jacqueline would have never betrayed her. The other being that the next time she saw Jacqueline, she would kill her without any remorse or restraint.

"Fuck!" she heard Samuel groan in pain behind her. She turned to see him crouched on the floor with a sword in his hand, coughing up blood. Ezekiel stood over him, looking down on his brother with a slight disgust as he gripped his sword. This was the tenth consecutive mock battle Ezekiel had brutally beaten him in.

"That was an even worse effort than the last," Ezekiel said, disappointed.

"I'm not suited for the battlefield," Samuel complained.

"You have to be. We need as many men fighting on our side as possible," Ezekiel said.

Samuel gasped in pain, digging his sword into the ground as he used it to prop himself up on his feet.

"If there's any of the four virtues we should be enhancing within our souls before the Kingsclans arrive, it's ingenuity, not vitality," he argued. "That's how we will stand a chance against their armies with ours, despite their superior numbers."

"You have enough ingenuity. If our training today is anything to go by, your vitality desperately needs work. Your vital essence is certainly not at the level a clan leader's should be," Ezekiel insulted.

Grace saw contention about Samuel's face. He bit the inside of his cheek as he did whenever someone had insulted him, but he could not think of a clever retort. Though he knew it was true, she could tell he did not appreciate hearing it in the slightest.

"I'm aware my vitality is lacking. You don't have to be harsh," Samuel said back. "Besides, I could say the same about your ingenuity."

Ezekiel clashed his sword against the sword Samuel was leaning on, digging it out from the grass and causing him to fall face-first into the mud.

"How's that for ingenuity?" Ezekiel scoffed.
He chuckled to himself maliciously as he walked to another side of the yard. He found the bark of the great tree to be a better sparring partner than his younger brother. Samuel picked himself and his sword up in shame.

"Where's Promise?" Grace asked in an attempt to distract her brother from the shame.

Samuel shrugged. "She's probably avoiding having to train with Mr Vitality," he sneered in reference to their tree-hacking brother.

Grace smirked at the jest. She dropped her bow and arrow and left to search for her.

***

Grace entered the front room, where one of the Hustan defenders told her they last saw Promise. Since their return to the Hustan, the space was cleared of all the old scrolls Samuel left lying around there and further decorated with shiny blades on the walls and dusted books adorning the fireplace and tables.

Grace saw her younger sister sitting in the weathered family chair with the baby Joseph in her arms. A welcome surprise that put a smile on her face. Another surprise stood a good distance away from Promise and her baby, one that filled Grace with less joy by the portraits and fireplace. A couple with moods as damp and grey as the dark-river-coloured armour they wore. She was in the downcast presence of Jean and Marie Irie.

"Good afternoon, Mr and Mrs Irie," Grace greeted the Arisclan couple.

"Afternoon, Grace," Jean greeted. Marie ignored her.
The Irie leaders hardly regarded Grace, their gazes locked on their grandson. Promise tickled her baby's belly, creating a choir of childish giggles that warmed the room with better effect than the fireplace. Though no amount of youthful cheer seemed enough to lift the late Francis' parents out of the dark emotional hole where they resided.

"I'm sorry for your loss. May all the virtues be with you," Grace said to them with a respectful bow. Her condolences were met with blank frowns.

"Francis is in a better place now, most likely. Although there's no way of knowing, that's what we tell ourselves to make the pain feel less potent," Marie sighed dejectedly.

Promise looked up from baby Joseph to witness the despondent faces of her late husband's grieving parents. Her cheerful expression petered out. The change in atmosphere altered the baby's mood. The giggling infant boy silenced himself as if he knew what was being discussed.

"When will the funeral be held?" Promise asked them.

"Whenever this unfortunate debacle with your clan is resolved. *If* it ever is," Jean answered. "That's why we came here today. *Before* any major fallouts."

"Are you here to show your support?" Grace asked, jumping at the opportunity. "We could use the backing of a high-standing Arisclan connected to us. Especially one so beloved and highly respected."

"It's cruel to keep a mother away from her baby for too long," Marie said, gesturing at Joseph in Promise's hands. "That's the only reason we're here."

On that note, she walked over to Promise, urging her to hand the baby over. Promise held her child tight in defiance. She only handed the infant over once she saw the glare of his grandfather.

"Perhaps you'll see him again once all this nonsense with your clan has been dealt with," Jean said.

"Right," Promise said meekly, her voice faltering as a lady does when they are soon to cry.

The Irie clan leaders left the room without as much as a goodbye, taking the crying Joseph away from the Zhakkari sisters and hurrying out of their Hustan. Grace had it in her mind to scold them, but thought it better she did not. She attended to her sister, who had her face buried in her hands.

"There's no need to worry, you'll see him again," she assured her.

"Not if we're killed after the Kingsclans sweep through our lands!" Promise cried.

"That won't happen," Grace said as if the outcome were determined. "We won't let it."

***

Grace lay with only the shadows of night as company, her room pitch black but for a small flame lit on a match that she pinched between her fingers. She gaped into the heart of its minuscule flames as the events of the day ran through her mind. Particularly, the argument between her brothers about the virtues in their souls. Of all the four virtues, she identified regality as her strongest.

From a young age, Grace was acutely aware of her high levels of regality. Of all the Zhakkari children, she was the sibling with the confident demeanour of a distinguished royal. However, she also knew that her abundance of regality was part of what inspired Jacqueline's jealousy, part of what led to her shaming and detainment.

Grace thought of plans for vengeance. She wished to savagely kill her dear friend Jacqueline the second the chance was given to her. She wondered whether doing so would affect her virtue of justness. Instead of pontificating on this for a while longer, she put out the match and sought an early night's rest.

In a day and a half, they would have to face the Kingsclans in battle.

AN ARMY ASSEMBLED

EZEKIEL Zhakkari was no stranger to the types of celebrations that occurred before or after an important battle. The celebrations he found himself in the middle of the day before the Kingsclans were set to attack their lands were a strange variation of them.

As opposed to occupying a tavern, they occupied a savannah a mile away from Zhakkari land. Instead of enjoying alcoholic beverages from rum to wine, they ate meat and made a ritual of collecting the finest waters from the rivers to drown their appetites in. And finally, the most glaring difference of all, the men intertwined their celebrations with training, hosting continuous mock-battle tournaments as part of the key entertainment.

Ezekiel watched with a studious sternness as his fellow Clan Zhakkari warriors circled a platform of tawny grass and wilting bushes. Four men fought a simultaneous battle with one another on this platform.

Over the short period from their grandstand to the present moment, Ezekiel, with the help of Grace, convinced many members of Clan Zhakkari's warrior class to fight for them in battle. They now had enough men to at least stand a chance against the Kingsclans, though not nearly enough to match them in even combat.

The mock battle tournament confirmed some of Ezekiel's worries. It was bad enough that they were at a numerical disadvantage. A few of these warriors seemed rusty. They were not accustomed to battle due to having seen no serious conflict in a while, other than drunken tavern brawls.

The dancing half-naked women who would travel around these celebrations and accost the men arrived. They all walked past Ezekiel, offering to give dances to him first and foremost before any other warrior.

Ezekiel took no interest in any of the girls and waved the majority onwards. That was until one of them caught his interest for other reasons.

Ezekiel motioned at this particular woman, telling her to come sit on his lap. The woman happily obliged, planting herself with a gentle enthusiasm on his armour-plated thigh. Ezekiel leaned in towards her with intimacy. She anticipated a passionate kiss. The dancing girl was instead met with a calm whisper.

"Where have I seen you before?" Ezekiel asked.
Taken aback by his seriousness in tone, the woman fixed her eyes on his face as if to tensely revise it. Ezekiel revised her face in the same way, taking in every feature.

"You don't remember me, Ezekiel? How hurtful," the woman chuckled.

Her warm chocolate eyes with flecks of lighter shades danced with an underlying mischief. Those eyes belonged to exactly who Ezekiel had assumed.

"Deborah Lawal," he said with a rare warmth and desire. "When was the last time the two of us spoke?"

"The tumultuous years of our passionate teenage romances," Deborah recalled. She crept up on Ezekiel's lap.

"I'll need a fresh reminder," Ezekiel said coquettishly. Deborah needed no further prompting from him, taking one of his hands and placing it on her firm buttocks as he leaned into her for a fruitful embrace. The pair enjoyed each other's lips. Ezekiel could taste a sweet wine on her tongue as they kissed for a while.

They broke apart with the widest of grins of the lustful excitement that came with their being together again.

The fiery passion that boiled through Ezekiel's body cooled, leaving a more thoughtful and melancholic temperament in its place.

"I wanted to marry you in those days. You could have been a proud woman of the main Zhakkari family if so," he told her. "But you disappeared without a trace. You left me without a goodbye."

"My father was sick. Our family had to move to another land in hopes of the change in climate improving his health," Deborah explained to him. "But he died quickly after, and I had to spend my later years of adolescence in said land, up until very recently."

Ezekiel nodded, taking it all in. "And now you've returned to our clan. As a pleasure-dancer," he observed.

There was a hint of unspoken judgement about him that Deborah quickly noticed.

"I only dance if that's what you're asking," she clarified. "I'm a pleasure-dancer, not a pleasure-maiden."

"Interesting," Ezekiel said, making sure not to sound judgmental in tone this time.

Deborah smiled at Ezekiel, her mouth tight. She rose from his lap, shook her head, and blew him a kiss. Ezekiel said nothing else as she wandered off to re-join her dancing sisters in other parts of the savannah.

Ezekiel no longer wore a mask over his emotions as soon as Deborah was out of sight. An amalgamation of pity and disgust stained his countenance as he thought about her current state.

***

Images of their forefathers decorated all four corners of the room, leaving not a single portion of the wall bare. The Zhakkari brothers and six of their most trusted warriors occupied the stratagem-quarters of their Hustan that night.

Ezekiel and Samuel stood at the head of a shield-shaped war table. The grand painting of their golden-armoured grandfather and founder of the clan, Abel Zhakkari, hung behind them. The grey-haired, thick-bearded, and regal-faced depiction of the illustrious man watched over them as they discussed the battles that were to take place upon the Kingsclan army's arrival the next day.

"...and as aforementioned, the numbers disadvantage is our greatest issue. But I have a series of plans to make up for it and increase the probability of a successful campaign," Samuel explained as he leaned over the table. "We must focus on engaging them indirectly instead of directly. We shall split up into squads that flank them as they approach our land from the hills over the oasis. We shall use the bushes and forests as hiding places where we'll concentrate on targeted key members of their army in clusters through projectile and long-ranged attacks, making sure to either kill their lions or have the beasts abandon their riders. Then, we'll continuously divide and regroup as we cut them with quick strikes and retreat over and over again without ever participating in single combat."

114

Samuel took a deep breath and waited for feedback. His brother congratulated him with a heavy pat on the shoulder.

"Excellent ideas," Ezekiel said. "They should allow for a more even battle."

"How do the rest of you feel about this?" Samuel asked the others. He received no answers from the other warriors, only half-hearted nods and unthinking stares.

Ezekiel noticed a pair of warriors around the table's uncaring attitude towards Samuel's speeches, their eyes wandering elsewhere as he spoke. He slammed his fists on the table, forcing their attention over to him.

"Listen to my brother's plans," Ezekiel snapped. "His body may not be suited for the battlefield, but his mind might be all that stops us from losing our heads on it."

The warriors nodded in apologetic obedience, offering their undivided attention to Samuel. The third Zhakkari child let on an awkward, satisfied smile of thanks.

"Indirect engagement, flanking squads from out of greenery, key targets struck and forced away from their lions, long-range projectiles, and a continuous retreat and regrouping system whilst avoiding single combat," Samuel said, recapping his battle plans. "Does everyone understand what we are to do?"

The warriors nodded, this time in genuine comprehension. Samuel nodded too as he stared into the vacant space ahead. Ezekiel could tell the specific minute details of the plans he laid out were somersaulting through the thirdborn's mind.

His brother's inner machinations were halted by the pounding of the door. Ezekiel grunted with frustration as he went to open it. He was met with a young Clan Zhakkari warrior whose armour showed signs of recent wear and tear.

"Ezekiel, sir. The Kingsclan armies!" the warrior panted, barely getting the words out.

"Yes, we're making plans for their attacks tomorrow. Leave us," Ezekiel dismissed.

"I'm afraid your preparations are futile, sir," the warrior gulped. "They've already started the attacks! The Osei and Khoza forces maraud through our lands as we speak!"

Collective shock marked the faces of those around the shield table. The warriors, previously confident with the plans moving forward, became ill at ease. Samuel bit the inside of his cheek hard enough to draw blood.

Ezekiel's usual undaunted demeanour failed to stand strong in light of the news. He sighed out of his nose, his mouth a twisted grimace.

"Christian Osei said he'd wait two days for our decision," Samuel sighed with frustrated disbelief.

"He fucking lied," Ezekiel growled.

***

The warriors of Clan Zhakkari were unable to execute Samuel's plans effectively on such short notice. They made strained efforts to defend their land as Clans Osei and Khoza pillaged through it.

Hundreds of men in gem-adorned armour of Hustan and crown emblems tore through the villages and farmlands on lion-back, cutting down every Zhakkari civilian they came across. Stone houses were being reduced to rubble, tavern-keepers were shot through the heart with arrows, and mothers and fathers were stabbed with daggers.

Clan Zhakkari warriors attempted to flank and isolate specific Osei and Khoza warriors whilst simultaneously trying to kill off the pillagers that desecrated their villages. Their success waned on both fronts. Blood sprayed, children were torn, screams resounded through the air over their land. Utter decimation of Zhakkari folk was in order.

Christian Osei parted his way through the main village, not even bothering to dismount his slowly moving lion. With a bored, dispassionate way about him, he rode through the villages. His longsword sliced down anything he came across, from warriors to civilians to livestock.

In an ironic fashion, Ezekiel disregarded the plans he had forced the other warriors around the table to pay attention to. His younger brother's tactics slipped out of his mind as he defaulted to base impulse. He fought the way he knew best. Unrepentant, straightforward brutality of the grizzliest order.

Ezekiel buried his battle-axe into the skull of the first Kingsclan soldier he found attempting to burn a cornfield. He exhaled sharply, sprinting with purpose as he ran to confront a cluster of seven of William Khoza's clan's soldiers further into the corn. Three other Clan Zhakkari warriors followed him for backup.

"Die bastard!" Ezekiel screamed.

He caught his first victim by surprise, carving across his chest with a battle-axe blow. He followed up with a strike to the second man, who deflected his attack with a parry of his longsword. As Ezekiel engaged in a bladed conflict with him, the three other Zhakkari warriors dealt with the remaining five corn-field-burning warriors of Clan Khoza.

Ezekiel's opponent proved to be more formidable than most he faced, able to continue parrying each of his strikes with skilful swordplay. With a suave deflection of the dozenth brutal axe attack, he manoeuvred Ezekiel to the side, allowing him to slash the Zhakkari on the side of his body where his armour was exposed.

Ezekiel unsheathed his two-pronged dagger in exasperated anger, wielding both it and his axe in tandem as he pressed forward with more strikes. His teeth clenched, nostrils flared, eyes bulged, and veins protruded.

He cut with violent determination. He sent unrelenting smite after smite the Khoza warrior's way. The cocky young man struggled to keep up as he deflected each hit with increasing difficulty.

Ezekiel paused his attacks to take a deep breath and regain his footing. The Khoza warrior saw this as an opportunity to go on the offensive. A plunge through the heart with two blades brought his efforts to a standstill.

Ezekiel twisted the blade as he watched a fountain of blood spill from the Khoza warrior's mouth.

The Kingsclan soldier buckled and dropped, to Ezekiel's great delight. The eldest Zhakkari continued to hack at his dead victim's body until his axe split him in two.

Ezekiel was invigorated. The vitality in his soul was strong and desperate to be put to use in protecting his land and people. He looked to see how his men were faring in their battles against the other Clan Khoza men.

He saw all three of his side's warriors lie either heavily wounded or stone-cold dead. An empty pain stirred in the pit of this stomach.

Ezekiel's instincts saved his life as he ducked underneath a swipe of a sword coming from behind him. He spun around to face another Khoza warrior in battle.

The Kingsclan warrior delivered the most powerful blow Ezekiel had ever experienced as a warrior, cutting him across his entire body before he could even blink in the man's direction. In a split second, a deep wound tracking from Ezekiel's left shoulder blade to the right side of his lower torso had been delivered.

Ezekiel fell like a heavy corpse being dropped into the sea. He lay amongst the cut-down corn, unresponsive. Permanently scarred, his body was losing blood as fast as his mind was losing consciousness.

What he last remembered that day was being lifted as dark shadows clouded his vision. The smell of smoke filled his nostrils. The footsteps of Kingsclan warriors filled his ears as they marched onwards to destroy his land.

AN ABYSMAL NIGHT

PROMISE Zhakkari's gentle brown eyes were tinted orange as the sight of immense fires filled them wholly. She sat at the back of a carriage with scorched burn marks on the wood, drawn by the beast with moulting fur.

Grace was outside the carriage, filling up the middle compartment with as many Zhakkari possessions as possible. Paintings, books, weapons, jewels, portions of meat, water, and anything she was able to get a grasp of beforehand.

As Grace frantically prepared for their impromptu departure, Promise's neck strained from looking back at their Hustan. Their great family home had been officially occupied by Osei and Khoza Kingsclan forces, who burned it down after picking it apart. Promise had seen Osei men destroy the structural integrity of the building with swords, axes, and spears, breaking off chunks of brick as it slowly fell to pieces. Khoza men took these bricks and threw them into the fires that lit up the fields behind the Hustan.

Promise winced with deep displeasure. She could not decide whether to keep her eyes forward or look back. The scene drew further away from her line of vision as Grace took hold of the reins and whipped the moulting lion into an onward charge.

"What about Samuel and Ezekiel?" Promise asked, fretting as the distance between their carriage and the destroyed Zhakkari land increased.

"I couldn't find them anywhere on the battlefield," Grace lamented with a sigh. "I'd like nothing more than for us to search for longer, but we haven't the time. All we can do is hope they've escaped."

The sweat of stress and strife marked the youngest Zhakkari's forehead as the prospect of her brothers' potential demise claimed a solid position in her mind.

She set her sights forward, gulping down a thick lump in her throat as she forced herself not to cry.

***

Christian Osei basked in the rays of the rising sun, enjoying the aftermath of his successful sweep through Zhakkari land. The most powerful man in Civcaz felt twice as such.

He stood upon a hill of charred grass and overlooked what used to be the main village. Lifeless and empty, no people roamed the streets. Most of the buildings were broken down, pieced apart, and had their remains scattered across the fields. He sighed with contentment, taking in the wake of his destruction with a serene gratitude.

To his left was his wife, Florence. Whilst he took in the sights of his victory, she took in the sight of him, not blinking once in a loving daze.

William Khoza approached the couple, scaling the hill with a scroll in hand. "My noble Osei," he called out as he arrived between them.

Christian and his wife attended to him with an impatience only subtly hidden. Less so on the latter's part.

"Yes?" Christian answered with a raised eyebrow.

"The other members of the Shared Council would like to know what plans you have relating to the Zhakkaris," William Khoza said.

"Can't this wait?" Florence pouted like a petulant teenager as she latched onto her lordly husband's arms. "We're enjoying a moment."

Florence squeezed Christian's arm tighter, adoring the feeling of being pressed against the hard biceps under his armour as she smiled up at him with wonder. Christian reciprocated no such affection, brushing her off. He removed her hand from his and focused solely on Khoza.

"I've been in talks with leaders of Saxe-Barbarian factions. Some of them have grown weary of the sea and are looking for places to station themselves. I've allowed them to stay on Civcaz soil as long as it's Zhakkari land. For a price, of course," Christian answered.

"Oh, right," William muttered, nonplussed. "I was of the impression that the Saxe-Barbarian idea was a potential suggestion. A rumination. I wasn't aware it was to be an actionable plan."

Christian's eyebrows furrowed, his forehead wrinkling in irritation at William's perplexed reluctance. "Are you saying you're not fond of my plans, Khoza?"

"I suppose I am to a certain extent, but I don't mean to offend you," William admitted to him in a brief panic. "I just can't hold my tongue and pretend I'm fine with Saxe-Barbarians staying on our land. They're lawless savages with violent customs and obscene sexual practices."

Khoza's honesty in his distaste for his plans mitigated the Osei leader's irritation. "Very true. But what better way to reform them than to take them onto Civcaz land? Perhaps we could teach them our customs," Christian proposed. "We could also use the money, don't you think? Especially with the Zhakkari's no longer being a source of land income as a Commonsclan. You don't want our land's gold reserves to suffer because of your irrational fear of a little sea faction, do you, Khoza?"

From a mere glance at his face, one could tell William was almost certainly not on board with anything Christian proposed. Yet this time, despite having said he would not moments ago, he held his tongue and accepted his idol leader's choices.

"Speaking of the Zhakkaris," Florence chimed in. "I heard the sibling quartet escaped after we destroyed their land. Shouldn't we be expelling forces to hunt them down and bring them to justice?"

Christian shook his head with a condescending flair.

"No. As long as they stay exiled and off Civcaz's main lands, it's better to leave them alive and out of sight. We can create a culture where we paint the Zhakkari as an ever-present threat to the sanctity of our lands. The rare few who sight them will keep the mainland civilians on high alert."

"Just as we did with Clan Godwin," William observed. Christian nodded concordantly. "Just as we did with Clan Godwin," he repeated with a smirk.

**

As was customary in times of turmoil, sweet dreams of times long gone populated Promise's mind as she slept. The nostalgic, recurring solace of the day of her wedding to the late Francis Irie.

All the staples of her subconscious escape were present. The Zhakkari men and women happily mingling with their Arisclan Irie counterparts, her handsome and noble Francis' eyes coloured by love and pride, her siblings setting aside their constant vitriol, Samuel and Grace's rare sweetness to

123

each other, Ezekiel's rarer, delightful disposition, and a wish in her heart that the day would never end.

But even her dreams could not act as a place of solace. All of a sudden, the very fabric of this sweet reality deteriorated in her mind. The version of herself within the dream blinked once, and the scenes around her changed.

The Arisclan Irie men and women were cutting and maiming their Clan Zhakkari counterparts with rusted blades. Her husband, Francis, was nowhere to be seen. Her siblings devolved into a bloody mess.

Grace's body shrivelled to an emaciated pile of weakness as she crouched over two bodies drenched in a pool of blood. One was Samuel with his head sliced open, and the other was Ezekiel with his heart ripped out.

Promise woke up violently, feeling as if her heart and mind were going to give out on her. Though it was all her body wanted to do, she was resilient in making sure she did not fall asleep again for a while. This was an easy task considering her whereabouts.

Promise's bed was the worn-out seats of her carriage and a blanket filled with holes. Her bedroom was a damp cave on the side of a mountain. She and Grace had spent the day travelling up a narrow path on the side of the craggy elevation in search of a place to hide, no longer having the strength to keep travelling on their journey of escape.

Grace sat awake on a small crater in the cave floor, eyes bloodshot, arms crossed. The same position Promise saw her in when she went to sleep hours prior.

Her older sister had the opposite reaction to her when it came to suffering from depressed despondency. During the days they travelled in search of a place to hide, Promise could not remember seeing Grace sleep once.

"Go to bed, Grace," Promise advised.

"I'm not in the mood for rest," Grace said, her voice low and serious.

"You can't stay up thinking all night. I won't have it," Promise demanded, a motherly way about her. "I still don't know whether my brothers are alive or not. I'm not having my sister die before I find out."

Grace groaned. She lay her body down on the cold, moist cave floor.

Promise kissed her teeth. "Don't be silly, Grace. Lie with me in the chariot-"

"It's over," Grace interrupted.

"Sorry?" Promise asked.

"It's over. We've truly lost everything this time," Grace lamented, staring into a crevice that gave her a glimpse of the night sky. "And this time, I have no idea how we're to recover. No idea at all."

Promise dearly wished to dismiss the pessimistic doom that was hanging in the air. She racked her brain to come up with any positive notions to dispel her sister's woes.

"At least we still have each other," she said, all she could come up with in that bleak cave of absent hope.

A BROTHER'S ABSENCE

SAMUEL Zhakkari paced back and forth under the leaky roof of a six-foot-high, three-foot-wide man-made shelter, constructed at the edge of a dead pasture from scrap metal and discarded waste. His brother sat behind him by a wall cushioned by a bed of old clothes.

Ezekiel had spent almost no time with his eyes open those days. He was constantly at rest in a near-comatose state. Heavy bandages wrapped around the eldest Zhakkari's body and torso, soaking up the blood from the deep wounds he had been given on the battlefield the day the Kingsclans destroyed their land.

Whilst the battle was taking place, Samuel had been waiting in the stratagem-quarters when a pair of Zhakkari warriors brought his bleeding brother in front of him on the shield table, with the deep wounds on show. He only had a few minutes to bandage them up.

Soon after, Osei and Khoza men broke down the Hustan defences, storming it and forcing him to make a hasty exit. Samuel was forced to carry an unconscious Ezekiel to a chariot. He rode off that day, hoping his sisters were able to do the same.

Weeks had passed since then. Aside from foraging for food and nursing Ezekiel back to health, Samuel had done nothing but hide in this scrap structure of theirs.

He paced through the small room as he thought of what on Earth he could do to climb the Zhakkaris out of the monumental hole of despair they were stuck in.

"Samuel," he heard his brother groan in deep pain.

That seemed to be all Ezekiel was able to do to express himself in his current state.

Usually, that tone of a groan meant he needed either water or food, neither of which they were blessed with having much of.

Samuel left their shelter for another forage.

***

Samuel traversed the edge of a deep lake with a sack of berries and items hanging around his neck by a string. The ominous waters were nigh-impossible to see through.

The sinister-appearing lake was the closest body of water he could find for miles that was fresh and clean. It was the closest oasis this abandoned land had to offer.

The water of the lake seemed strange to Samuel as he arrived. It was mostly still, yet with the occasional ripple of waves bubbling through it. Somehow, it seemed unnatural. Ignoring his wariness, Samuel took a rudimentary clay-made chalice out of the sack he carried with him and started to collect water.

As Samuel filled the clay container with water, the unnatural ripples reverberated through the lake with a higher frequency. Had they stopped there, he would have paid no mind to them and continued collecting. But as the ripples grew in size, range, and doubled in frequency, so did his level of concern.

127

The water in front of Samuel burst into an exploding fountain of blackened moisture. A man emerged from beneath the rippled waves. The man's crazed smile, sharp cutlasses equipped as if ready for battle, and tattered blue cloth in lieu of armour were recognisable. Samuel was well aware of the class of man he was encountering.

Seven eruptions of water burst around Samuel as crooked-toothed men of matching garbs emerged from under the lake's ripples. He was surrounded by outlaws of the seas. Saxe-Barbarians.

The man in front of Samuel lunged forward at a blistering speed, grabbing his hands and dunking him into the water. Samuel's berry and water sack was emptied and forced over his head as the barbarians cackled.

***

Following an hour of muffled struggling that was met with beatings to the body, and an hour after that marked by a quiet acceptance of his fate, Samuel had the sack removed from his head. The minuscule air holes that had been poked into the bag by the barbarians were barely enough to keep him conscious. He gasped for gulps of air as he checked his surroundings in a blurred frenzy.

The group of Saxe-Barbarians circled him, smiling with anticipation. Samuel avoided all of their gazes and studied the black, smoky enclosure around them.

From the faint markings on each wall and the ceiling, he could tell this room used to be part of a stronghold or the stratagem-quarters of a clan, perhaps one that was long gone. He could also tell that the walls were not black when they were built. They were burnt, presumably by the Saxe-Barbarians who circled him.

"Is there a reason you barbarians took me home like I'm one of your sea bitches?" Samuel asked irreverently, trying to mask the fear pulsing through him.

The men in saxe-coloured armour cackled in amusement at his joke as he put on a fake smile.

Samuel's smile dropped, being replaced with churning concern as the barbarians stopped encircling him. They stood still in an uneven formation with wider smiles.

He stared ahead at two of the men who stood right in front of him and noticed a third approaching from the back of the room. The man moved past his comrades to face Samuel directly.

The latest member of this group of barbarians was a man he had not seen at the lake. Shorter and considerably more muscular than the others, with dreadlocked hair and intact saxe armour, he stood out to Samuel as being above them. A leader of the faction.

The leader wore an odd half-smile on his face and a golden trinket in the socket of his left eye.

"Are you the boss?" Samuel asked, struggling to maintain his faux-irreverence.

"I am, yes. I'm flattered you noticed so quickly," the golden-eyed man quipped back. "You used to be somewhat of a boss yourself. You're Samuel, aren't you? Of the former Commonsclan Zhakkari."

Samuel could no longer keep his irreverence. He quailed at the sound of his name coming out of this golden-eyed outlaw's mouth. He had not a single clue as to why this barbarian would know his name and bring him here.

"Who are you?" he asked.

"Gideon. Gideon Goldensight," the leader of the Saxe-Barbarians said, introducing himself.

Samuel gestured at the trinket in his eye socket. "I can see why," he scoffed.

"Yes, you're very observant," Gideon chuckled. "Not observant enough to avoid capture, though."

Samuel sat there with a bothered expression as the barbarians laughed in his face.

"From what I heard, you Saxe-Barbarians populated the seas, not lakes. How was I to know of your shameful drop in station?" Samuel retorted.

The barbarians laughed. Samuel realised they were inclined to laugh at any joke made in their presence, whether it was funny or not. Or whether it was made at their expense or not.

"Our living situations have changed in general. Some of our men have been allowed to buy settlements and station themselves on the lands of Civcaz. They've been permitted by Christian of Kingsclan Osei himself," Gideon informed, much to Samuel's surprise. "Ironic. He's the same man who is responsible for you and your family no longer being allowed on Civcaz. That must be why you're spending your time wading through lakes in distant lands."

Samuel clenched his jaw, controlling the fury that the mention of Osei stirred within him. "Is that why you've captured me? To repay your debt to him by serving me on a platter?" he asked.

"No. I'm taking you somewhere actually worth the journey," Gideon Goldensight laughed. "You'll make a fine spectacle for the boys on board."

Samuel caught one final glimpse of the barbarian leader's twinkling golden eye as the sack went over his head again. He wondered where he would be taken this time.

***

The next time the sack was removed from Samuel's head, he was faced with more Saxe-Barbarians. He found he was standing on a beach of rough sand that, for reasons unknown to him, seemed to burn the souls of his bare feet.

He saw that the man who removed the sack from his head was many paces away from him and running. The man bounded up a walkway that took him onto a sizable brigantine ship with wide saxe-coloured sails. Twenty-one other barbarians waited on the ship, howling and hollering at Samuel. Gideon Goldensight led the chants.

"Men, why don't we play a little game of *pin the blade on the Zhakkari*?" Gideon asked his fellow sea-faring savages. "The first one to earn a taste of his Civcaz blood gets to keep *all* the diamonds we stole from Barbsav!"

The twenty-one barbarians unsheathed their cutlasses as they jumped off the ship with reckless abandon. Samuel backed away slowly.

"You need to start running!" Gideon advised him.

A SISTER'S CHANGE

GRACE Zhakkari felt as if she was no longer herself. She sat in a chariot, calcifying with dirt in the cave that was their new home. She had neither the energy nor the desire to do anything but stare at the stalactite ceilings for hours on end.

When staring at the ceiling bored her, she would watch whatever her younger sister kept herself busy with.

That day, Promise used a pin and a cloth to sew up the holes in their blankets. The day before, she washed their clothes, and the day before that, she collected meat and fruit from foraging outside. Her industriousness pleasantly surprised Grace.

During their last unofficial exile, after the death of her husband, all Grace could remember Promise wanting to do was sleep the days away. There were a couple of days in which she defaulted to that, but on the whole, Promise seemed almost *too* high-functioning.

Grace could only wonder if Promise's mind had cracked under the pressure. This constant busyness of her sister struck her as a form of strange psychotic break that allowed her to ignore the severity of their situation and suppress the emotions that came with it.

Grace watched in wonder, hardly believing that her little sister was sound enough to whistle as if all was right.

"Everything alright?" Promise asked her, stopping her work mid-whistle.

"Yes, all things considered," Grace sighed.

Promise smiled, returning to her sewing. Psychotic break or not, Grace appreciated Promise's strange turn of optimism. It kept that dwindling hope within that was precariously dangling off a ledge from swan-diving into despair. All was not lost just yet.

The universe must have been toying with Grace. Minutes after she had decided that all might be well, a sign was sent that it would not be. Measured footsteps echoed from around the corner as the two sisters looked towards the cave entrance.

In the weeks they had been holed up on the side of that mountain, only two other living people had occupied it aside from them. None had gotten this close to confronting them. None until that moment.

A tall man made himself known, entering the cave with his face partially covered by the shadows of the deflected, dull sunlight peeking through the mountain crevice. He stepped forward, the shadows uncovering his face to reveal uneven prickly skin, an unkempt beard, and dull eyes.

Grace stepped out of the carriage and walked over to where Promise was sitting. She protected her sister as the man came closer. "Can we help you, sir?"

The words had hardly escaped Grace's mouth when the scraggly man rushed towards her, ducking low. Grace no longer possessed the energy needed for any strength or reaction time that would have prevented this man from tackling her to the ground. He pinned Grace down to the cave floor. Promise dived out of the way, leaving her sister to be mauled as she rushed towards the chariot.

"If you want your face uncut, give me all that's in your possession! Food! Water! Fucking everything!" the man rambled in a mouth-foaming craze as he scratched and beat at her body.

"Unhand me now, you revolting bastard!" Grace screamed in futile defiance.

The man ignored her, digging his nails into her flesh as he tore at her clothes in a debased attack. Grace grappled with the man painfully, losing the struggle as he clawed at her with unmatched zeal.

"Ah! Fuck! Fuck! Fuck! Fuck! Fuck!" the man screamed all of a sudden. To her surprise, he let go, releasing her instantaneously.

The revolting attacker leapt off of Grace and patted at his neck, his face distorted and his body a dancing spectacle as he pranced in excruciating pain. Grace assumed this to be a mental illness or perhaps a sporadic seizure. That was until she took notice of two things.

Firstly, she noticed a pool of blood dripping from a quickly corroding crater of flesh on the back of his neck. Secondly, she noticed Promise. The young mother stood behind him with a metal container of a dark purple liquid in her shaking hands.

"Horrid bitch!" the man screamed.

He turned to throw more insults at Promise, who threw something back in turn. The purple liquid made contact with the violent, rabid man once more, scarring his face beyond repair. His eyes were burned shut, his skin was broken down, and his mouth was reduced to a mutilated mess of hanging, meaty flesh.

The man gargled with incoherent agony as pieces of his face fell like they were made of clay. Grace covered her mouth, gulping to prevent the vomit that had been stirring in her from erupting at the sight.

Pieces of flesh broke off the man's face, another bloody crater forming where his nose and mouth once were. The crater deepened until you could see the bones of his skull.

Promise watched the man twitch and die with a righteous stillness. She fastened the lid on the metal container of the deadly purple concoction. With the man having finally succumbed to his agonising death, Promise stepped over his body and walked to return the container underneath the carriage.

Grace stared in shocked horror as her sister casually moved on from the scene.

"What in all the fucking souls and virtues of the Earth was that?!" she questioned in exclamation.

"A few days ago, I found a series of potions in a container with some notes among the items you packed in the chariot. They helped me make *that*. It must have been part of an experiment Samuel was carrying out in the stratagem-quarters a while ago," Promise explained.

"And why did you see it fit to make something like that?!" Grace asked.

Promise pointed at the dead man. "For situations like this," she asserted.

Grace looked over the melted physiognomy of the man, imagining the amount of pain he must have gone through in his final moments. She did not feel sorry for him, reasoning that he had to die as soon as he attacked her. Still, she felt as if a knife to the heart, a slice of the throat, or even a brutal suffocation would have been more humane.

"Was that your first kill?" Grace asked.

Promise released a deep sigh in tandem with a heavy nod.

"It was," she admitted. "In fact, I think he's the first person I've ever attacked."

Grace looked at the dead man again, baffled that her baby sister was capable of such violence. "Promise, you shouldn't feel the need to do things like this."

"And why not? I received no physical training from our father. I can't wield a blade or throw a punch. Why shouldn't I find other ways to kill those who attack us?"

"Because it's not in your nature! It's not in your constitution!" Grace argued. "Father didn't refuse to give you physical training as a slight! You're better than this, Promise. Sweeter than this."

Promise shook her head in emphatic disagreement.

"It's no secret that I'm the weak sibling. Samuel has his wits, Ezekiel has his strength, and you're one of the most capable people I know. In comparison, I'm useless. I've always been useless. Fundamentally *useless*," she said with pain in her voice.

Grace frowned. Hearing her little sister speak of herself in such a manner hurt her heart. Growing up, she never realised that Promise had felt that way or had any reason to. But now it was as clear as day.

"I've been weak, too weak. I should have been preparing my mind and body for these dangers like the rest of you," Promise continued. "Perhaps if I had been before, we Zhakkaris would have been a stronger, more united front. My husband would be alive, my baby would be with me, and our lands wouldn't have been destroyed."

Promise stormed away from her older sister and returned to her sewing station. She fixed their clothes and blankets in a frustrated huff.

Perturbed by her reasoning, Grace loured at her sister. Yet instead of using the passionate counterarguments that ran through her head, she left the matter to rest.

She could not, with honest conviction, claim that what Promise had said was wrong.

**

Hours had passed since Promise's acidic killing of the rabid man and their subsequent argument. Hours that the sisters spent in silence.

Grace lay in the chariot, staring at stalactites. Promise went to another section of the cave to ration their food for the coming week. An undisturbed quiet held within the mountain cave. A quiet that was soon to be disturbed.

It seemed to be the female Zhakkari pair's unlucky day. They received yet another unwanted visit in their crevice abode. Yet another person travelled up the mountain and stumbled upon them.

"My soul! Those mad wanderers were actually *right*!" exclaimed a laughing female voice. "The mountains *are* suffering from a Zhakkari infestation."

Grace thought her mind was playing tricks on her. The face she knew belonged to that voice was imprinted in her head, yet as she slowly turned to check, she could not half believe it. Two Arisclan defenders of lioness-emblemed armour stood at the entrance to the cave, accompanying the highly familiar face and voice. Ahead of her, Grace saw her former friend and the source of all of her recent revenge fantasies. Jacqueline Bello.

The sullen face she associated with her treacherous former companion was no longer her main form of countenance. Jacqueline wore the same smug superiority that Grace had seen a brief glimpse of the night she lied to the Kingsclan defenders about the Zhakkari family's crimes.

Grace stepped out of the chariot and walked forward, coming closer to Jacqueline. She made sure to keep a fair distance between the two of them when she faced her. Not out of a fear of her or the defenders she brought for protection, but out of wariness of what she might do if she were to get her hands on the traitor.

"Congratulations, you've found me," Grace spat sardonically. "What do you fucking want?"

"That's not how *I* would speak to a former friend," Jacqueline mocked.

"I don't consider lying traitor cunts friends of mine, former or otherwise," Grace asserted.

A tight smile was all Jacqueline could muster to mask her resentment of the female Zhakkari's hostility.

"I came here to apologise," Jacqueline sighed. "I'm sorry for what happened between us that day."

A half-baked apology if Grace had ever heard one.

"Is that all? Is that what you tracked me down all the way here for?" she scoffed.

Jacqueline wagged her finger, tutting at her like a pedagogue. "I also came here to give you an offer," she said. "One that I think you'll struggle to refuse."

Grace's curiosity overrode her anger as she took another step closer to the Bello.

"Ever since your exile, Clan Bello's influence has increased. Especially in the eyes of the Kingsclans, you'll be happy to hear," Jacqueline gloated. Grace was, in fact, not happy to hear that. "My words contributed to your detainment and exile. They could easily be used to reverse it, should I feel it necessary."

"More lies from a virtueless bitch," Grace scoffed in response, livid at the fact that Jacqueline would poison her ears with such blatant falsehoods.

"My mother, father, and brother still hold love in their hearts for you. Especially my brother. The entire Bello family has spoken on behalf of your character, and because of their speeches, the lands are considering a pardon."

"A pardon for the Zhakkaris as a whole?" Grace asked.

"No, not for the rest of your family. Our influence won't stretch so far," Jacqueline said. "The pardon would be for you and you alone."

Grace studied Jacqueline's face. She did not believe her, but if she had to bet her life on whether she was lying or not, she would not be able to wager the gold.

"All of what you're saying is nothing but rotten lion shit," Grace asserted, feigning certainty.

Jacqueline folded her arms. "Is what I've said so hard to believe? Have you forgotten how much the people of my clan love you? My mother and father used to gush over you as if you were a child of their own. My brother scoffed when I said I wanted to perform at a gala, as he knew it wouldn't be right to deprive our people of your grace and beauty on stage!" she scoffed in explanation, her envy seeping through her praise. "You're loved in Clan Bello, and although you were accused of conspiring with your brother, you weren't accused of committing any crimes yourself. Do you *honestly* not believe that we could have arranged a pardon for you?"

Jacqueline's speech had not completely swayed Grace. It had not completely failed either. She watched her friend eye her with silence. Grace made sure her mouth was fastened shut, her lips not moving to even take a breath. Though she refused to say anything, her eyes told all. One look into them delighted Jacqueline, prompting her first genuine smile since her arrival at the cave.

Jacqueline retrieved a golden coin with a lioness emblem from behind her back. She flicked it into Grace's catching hands.

"The next time you find yourself on Clan Bello land, use that to pay for something in a village. The people will know you're accepting the potential pardon, and you'll be brought to our Hustan for a talk," Jacqueline explained. "I hope to see you very soon."

Jacqueline turned and exited the mountain cave, taking her Arisclan defenders with her and leaving Grace with much to think about. Grace sighed.

"You don't believe she's being genuine?" she heard Promise ask. She saw her little sister walking out of another section of the cave with a container of food and a sour face.

Grace gave Promise no answer. She could not, with honest conviction, determine whether she did or did not.

A MAN'S WORSHIP

EZEKIEL Zhakkari laboured through the pains of his aching body. He ignored the stinging burns of the scarcely healed wounds that scarred it deep beneath his bandages. He walked a long journey, looking past perished pastures and towards a blackening lake.

A day and a half had gone by since he had last seen Samuel. His time in this foreign land had been spent drifting in and out of consciousness as his younger brother nursed him back to health, tending to his bandages and retrieving his food and water. A shameful state of affairs, Ezekiel thought, but a necessary one considering his condition.

Almost two moons ago, Samuel left to collect more berries and water as he would usually do. Only he would never be gone for a day. His absence for this length of time was unusual.

So, regardless of the heavy toll of pain getting up on his feet and walking for miles was causing him, Ezekiel would not rest until he located his brother and ensured his safety. One of his main search areas was this enormous black lake he was approaching.

***

Ezekiel found unexpected company in his search for his brother. A group of wanderers were wading through the black lake as he walked by it.

Six unassuming men ranging from middle-aged to elderly stepped their feet in and out of the water. Ezekiel thought nothing of these men and set out to avoid them as he looked for Samuel. Which he would have done, had he not heard one of them speak.

"Are you looking for your brother?" the most elderly of the men said. A man of feeble frame, jolly expression, and a head of hair so thick it would have seemed youthful if not for its stark whiteness. Alarm bells rang in Ezekiel's head as he approached the elder.

"What made you say that?" he questioned, staring down the man with a brutal scowl.

The Elder was not intimidated, nor did he feel confronted. He smiled at Ezekiel as he answered.

"A day ago, we saw a man captured at this lake from afar. You look and walk similarly to that man. As if you were him writ large," The Elder said. "I assumed you had to be some sort of companion of his. Probably a brother, considering your similarities. *And* considering the concern etched on your face."

Ezekiel tightened his face, scowling at the assumptions. Uneasiness plagued his soul at the hearing of them, as well as the word 'capture' being used.

"Where was the man taken?" he asked.

"I'm not sure. All we saw was that he was taken by Saxe-Barbarians," The Elder explained. "This happened less than two days ago. Perhaps you could still find them along the land's shores if you travel fast."

"Thank you for the information," Ezekiel said. With that, he made his way to leave the lake, trudging onwards.

As he was turning to leave, the elder could not help but notice the limp in Ezekiel's gait and the struggling breaths exhaled from his mouth with every step. As much as he desired to, the eldest Zhakkari could not hide his afflictions.

"I hope you're not planning on walking all through your search. You'll never find your brother in the state you're in," The Elder laughed as he watched him walk.

Ezekiel stopped. "I'm not exactly spoilt for choice when it comes to travel options, old man," he snarked, irritated that he even had to explain himself.

The Elder chuckled as he exchanged knowing looks with the other water-wading men.

"We have a carriage we could take you on. I'm sure my friends wouldn't mind a minor excursion if it means you'll find your brother," he said. The Elder's friends gave confirming nods.

Ezekiel levied a measured glance at the jovial elder and his friends. "What do you gain from this?" he asked in accusation.

The elder clutched his stomach with a laugh, hearty and true. "Can't people do things out of the kindness of their hearts anymore?" he asked.

***

Ezekiel had not heard much about Barbsav before he and his brother had escaped to that dead pasture. During his journey in the elder's carriage, he could see why.

The land was destitute. The fields were even drier than Zhakkari grass. The sunlight was pale, with the skies it beamed from permanently overcast. The forests were filled with wilting trees.

Later, they travelled along a shoreline. Ezekiel noted that he had not seen a single sign of civilisation on this land. Travelling wanderers and pillaging barbarians were all that populated this 'nation', if he could even call it one. The only landmarks of minor interest were the sandy beaches, which sizzled as the carriage wheels parted through them. He saw why Barbsav was called *Civcaz's suffering sister land*.

Ezekiel set his sights away from the surrounding lands and towards the elder. The old leader held hands with another wanderer, both of their eyes closed. Ezekiel saw, clasped within their intertwining hands, a crumpled-up piece of old scroll paper. The men interlinked with a violent bashing of their heads together that neither seemed to acknowledge the pain of. As they broke apart, Ezekiel realised what he had just witnessed. They completed an unorthodox form of virtuous worship ritual. A different version of what he remembered his father, Kingsley, doing before battles.

"You perform worship rituals for the four virtues?" Ezekiel asked.

"Multiple times per day," the elder informed him with a warm smile. Ezekiel felt a rare sensation of comparative inadequacy. Aside from the commemorative dinner he and his siblings held in honour of their late parents, Ezekiel had not actively worshipped the soul virtues in years.

"You don't see many people who still worship the four virtues daily," Ezekiel mentioned. "My father was the last man I knew who would as often as you claim."

"Your father was a wise man. It's good to enhance your soul as often as you can. It gives you the strength you need to deal with this life," The Elder said.

"My siblings and I didn't worship much ourselves, but he used to make sure we built the virtues in our souls regardless. He and my mother would say it was to help us prepare for any dangers to come," Ezekiel recalled fondly.

"They were correct. It's crucial for those who want to face the trials and tribulations of life in spirit to hold their virtues strong! That's what I tell my men, too," The Elder affirmed. "Especially with our current situation."

Their *current situation*. Ezekiel thought about this for a moment. Of all the types of people he had expected to see on abandoned Barbsav land, ritualistic wanderers of such a pious nature were an oddly common occurrence.

"What is a group of virtue worshipers doing so far from Civcaz land?" Ezekiel asked.

"I could ask you the same," said The Elder in retort. "My friend over there claims you are Ezekiel of Commonsclan Zhakkari. He says the man you're looking for is called Samuel."

The man riding the carriage forward on a striped leopard turned to give Ezekiel a wink. The eldest Zhakkari was not amused by the gesture.

"Answer my question first, then I'll answer yours," Ezekiel insisted.

"Very well," The Elder said, clearing his throat with a chuckle. "We were part of the worship class of people. Former peasants who were allowed to live in the same chambers where we performed rituals for people in the land. So, when the Kingsclans decided to get rid of many of our temples, we were without a home, without a clan, and thus were ushered off Civcaz land."

Ezekiel sat up in his seat, intrigued. "So, you were technically banished?" he asked. The Elder nodded. "We were quite literally banished. Our Commonsclan is not even a clan anymore."

"Why?!" The Elder asked, as concerned as if it were his family that had been brought down.

"Heinous crimes were pinned on my brother. Some exaggerated, most false. Murder that was only the result of righteous self-defence, a rape that never happened, treason that never transpired. All sorts that the rest of us were accused of helping him commit."

The Elder and his comrades' jolly natures dampened in solidarity with Clan Zhakkari's plight. "And you have faith in your brother? You are sure he did not commit these crimes?" he asked.

Ezekiel nodded with certainty. "Samuel wanted to improve our lands. He would never do anything to taint them. He joined the Kingsclan Shared Council with the expressed purpose of implementing policies that would enhance the virtues within the souls of the people. He was betrayed by Osei, Khoza, and the other council members."

"Your brother sounds very righteous," The Elder complimented.

"He is. *And* very intelligent," Ezekiel added. "If I had at least attempted to follow his battle plans, instead of impulsively throwing myself into war, I wouldn't have these tormenting scars."

Ezekiel pointed at the bandages that covered his body and torso to emphasise his point. The Elder's eyes seemed to light as they travelled across Ezekiel's bandages and back to his pensive gaze.

"You speak very kindly of your brother, Zhakkari," The Elder noted. "We'll make sure you reconnect with him. By fire or by force."

***

It was the time of day when Christian Osei would typically attend a royal Kingsclan luncheon. A time of day when he would be served by male and female surfs, both from Arisclans and Commonsclans, as he ate his fill.

He should have been surrounded by friends and family. Instead, he spent the afternoon alone by a solitary river piercing through a valley on Osei land. The most powerful man in all of Civcaz crouched by the flowing stream as a peasant child would.

Christian studied his reflection as if he had not seen it before that very moment. In place of the Osei armour he usually wore, he was dressed in simple tunic robes. Though he did keep his family gems adorned on his sleeves.

Christian had let his hair grow out further than usual in tufts of soft and fine yet scattered tight curls. He was a very handsome man with beautiful eyes, a wonderfully warm complexion, and a sharp jaw. He was blessed in this department, evident by the reflection staring back at him. Yet he looked at his reflection as if the image of a horrid creature was staring back at him.

Christian drew saliva from the back of his throat and spat it at his image in the river. He grumbled under his breath as he stood up with flair, swishing the robes of his tunics and leaving the valley in scorn.

***

Samuel lay hidden beneath a pile of leaves lining the ground of a wilted forest. Aside from the occasional break for meals and plunder, the barbarians did not give up their game. They would always return to the forest to search for him.

Since he first escaped into the forest, he refused to risk leaving it for fear of finding barbarians waiting for him on the other side. Using his wits, misdirection, and camouflage, he had avoided capture thus far. But with the empty hole in his hungry stomach and a fatigued mind marred by a lack of water and sleep, his wits were gradually leaving him.

The most Samuel could do was hide within the leaves and struggle to keep himself awake until he figured out a way to escape unnoticed.

A rustling sound forced Samuel's eyes wide open. His weakening mind prepared for another escape into another part of the forest, only to realise that he could not hear barbarian laughter. He took the leaves off his face and looked to see who was near him.

Samuel assessed that he could hardly trust his eyes, as he saw an apparition of his desires manifested. A burly mirage of a non-barbarian man who could rescue him.

It was not until he saw the apparition touch a wilted leaf that he realised it was not just a real man, it was the one man he wanted to see more than any other in the world.

"Ezekiel?!" Samuel uttered, straining his voice to get his attention.

Ezekiel's eyes shifted in Samuel's direction. He saw him a few trees into the distance, lying covered with leaves.

"This is where you wandered?" Ezekiel chuckled, delighted to see his brother again.

"I was captured by Saxe-Barbarians whilst fetching water for you at the black lake," Samuel coughed. "They're playing a cruel game with me. They gave me a chance to run before chasing after me with knives. If they find me, they'll kill me."

"I was aware of the first part. Not so much the second," Ezekiel mentioned. "But that hardly matters. We're leaving now," he said in a relieved whisper.

Ezekiel lifted his younger brother over his shoulders. He carried him on his back.

"Careful, Ezekiel. Your wounds haven't healed. You don't want to put any strain on your body," Samuel said.

"You've spent all this time taking care of me. It's time I returned the favour," Ezekiel retorted.

Samuel coughed, clearing his throat. "I suppose the more pertinent issue is, with both our ailments, how are we going to escape this forest quickly enough for no barbarians to happen upon us?"

Ezekiel smiled at his aching brother's remarks. "Don't worry about that," he said. "I've recently met a class of very good men who can help us."

***

Samuel felt a strange nostalgia as he lay next to Ezekiel. Crates were placed on top of them as they hid within the lower compartments of the carriage. It reminded him of a similar manoeuvre when they were sneaked back on Civcaz's mainland by Oliver Bala and his chicken coop.

Samuel peeked out of a hole in the carriage. He witnessed a group of barbarians re-enter the forest he and Ezekiel were being smuggled out of.

Once they left the forest behind them, the Zhakkari brothers were permitted to sit aboard the carriage amongst the wanderers. Samuel finally saw the jovial elderly face of the man who helped Ezekiel save him. Soon after, he listened to the same story the wanderers told his brother.

"You were practically exiled from Civcaz by the Kingsclans, too?" Samuel asked, following its conclusion.

"Exactly what I said," Ezekiel confirmed.

The Elder nodded. "Yes. Your family and my people suffered the same fate. We've both been resigned to the forgotten lands of Barbsav," The Elder noted. "It seems those who hold the four virtues in high regard are no longer welcome in Civcaz."

"That seems to be the case," Samuel said, his voice trailing off. He glared at nothing in particular, his face a warped sneer.

"What are your plans in terms of rekindling all that your family has lost?" The Elder asked him.

"Find our sisters. That's all we can do for the moment," Samuel lamented. "I haven't even the faintest clue as to how we could return to our old station."

"If you ever have a clue as to what you're going to do, you can count on our help," The Elder assured him. Samuel smiled with gratitude.

Ezekiel chuckled, imitating The Elder. If these wanderers were useful enough to help him locate his brother in only a few hours, he was sure they would do wonders in aiding their rise to their old station and then some.

A WOMAN'S WORD

PROMISE Zhakkari stared at her sister with caution. The two of them sat across from each other on the cave floor as they ate dry meat. A week in the past, Jacqueline Bello's visit was long enough ago to have been forgotten. Especially when daily survival in a mountain cave was one's top priority. Yet Promise could not help but think about it every time she sat with Grace.

"I hope you're not thinking of taking Jacqueline's offer," she commented as they ate.

"I'm not!" Grace exclaimed, offended that her sister took her for someone who would.

Promise's eyes narrowed by a millimetre. "You can understand my worry at your hesitation-"

Grace rose with righteous anger, startling Promise into closing her mouth and dropping her food.

"Never in my entire fucking life would I turn my back on family just to save my own skin like a virtueless cunt!" Grace shouted.

Her fists balled as if she were about to beat her sister. Promise would not utter another word on the topic. She hoped that she could trust Grace as she watched the second-born Zhakkari storm off in a huff.

Grace left the cave. She walked out onto the winding ledge that took you down to the midsection of the mountain. She paused her journey once she saw some men travelling up the winding rocks.

Her first instinct was to travel back to the cave and collect weapons in case these men were thieves or barbarians. Although as the men drew closer, she no longer feared their presence. She welcomed it, hurrying down to meet with them as soon as possible.

They were men she knew very well.

***

Minutes later, Promise saw her sister run back into the cave in a mood thousands of times brighter than the one she had left in. Grace squeezed Promise in the tightest hug she was capable of subjecting her to, strong enough to almost break her delicate ribs.

"They're here! They're alive! Thank the virtues of all men past and present, they're alive!" Grace cheered with tears in her eyes and a face-tearing smile of wondrous awe.

"Who's here? Who's alive?" Promise asked, though she assumed the answer. She looked to the cave entrance with excitement. Just as she expected, both her brothers came around the corner with smiles.

The sight of Ezekiel and Samuel was enough for Promise to momentarily forget all their woes. The gratitude she felt in their presence once more made her a contender for the happiest woman in the world award.

"Sisters," Ezekiel greeted with a casual smirk. Grace laughed with him.

"Ezekiel! Samuel!" Promise cheered as the Zhakkari siblings stood close to one another for the first time in a while. "How did you know we were here?"

"A group of wanderers helped us. They spread the word amongst all the wanderers in this land for days until they heard news about the sightings of two young Zhakkari women. Now, after days of gruelling searches, we've found you! We've finally found you!" Samuel gushed with the purest enchantment.

"Bless their souls for a hundred years to come!" Promise applauded.

Samuel's eyes danced around the intricacies of this cave that his sister had made into a home, from the markings on the mountain walls to the arrangement of dirty, stained, yet neatly organised items in the chariot.

"This place is much cosier than ours was," Samuel snorted as he glanced about.

"Where did you two stay?" Grace asked.

"The brilliant Samuel Zhakkari built a shelter for us out of scraps," Ezekiel said. "It was still better than sleeping in the wild," he added.

"But nowhere near as good as sleeping in a Hustan," Samuel said, diverting the topic of the conversation. "Now, our first order of business should be thinking of plans to restore our clan."

The siblings' cheerful, elated embraces of reunion came to an abrupt stop. The stark reminder of their current overall fate caused Ezekiel's jaw to tense, Promise's arms to cross, and Grace's eyes to grow cogitative.

"As our older brother over here once said, *what's there to think about*?" Grace answered, gesturing to Ezekiel. "We're going to fucking war over this."

Ezekiel grinned. "Yes. We are."

"Have you all gone mad?!" Promise asked, gasping.

"Not entirely," Ezekiel scoffed jokingly.

"How are we going to start another war against the Kingsclans after how the last one turned out?!" Promise asked. "Back then, we had a slightly smaller army, and we lost. This time, we don't even have an army to begin with!"

Samuel sighed. "You're right, we'll need to collect a lot of resources if we want to even think about war."

"Those wanderers said they'd help us with anything to do with restoring our clan," Ezekiel mentioned. "I reckon they could help us with this."

"I suppose that's the best we can do for now," Samuel said. "Let's bring them here. We'll conjure up a proper plan in our heads along the way."

"Who are these wanderers you keep speaking of?" Promise asked.

Her brothers gave no answers to her inquiring utterance, choosing to leave the cave and show her.

***

A quarter of an hour later, the brothers returned with a group of twenty or so men in pious cloaks, the leader of which was an elderly man with beautiful white hair.

"Zhakkari sisters," The Elder said, greeting them with a respectful tilting of his head. Grace and Promise reciprocated with tilted heads of their own.

"You're the people who've helped my brothers so much?" Grace observed as she looked over the series of bearded and weathered men.

"They're virtuous men who perform worship rituals to enhance their souls daily," Samuel said.

"Just like father did," Ezekiel said.

The doughy group of over-smiling men earned respect in both Zhakkari women's eyes as memories of their late patriarch flooded their minds.

"Why are Civcaz worshippers wandering around Barbsav?" Grace asked.

"The Kingsclans don't appreciate worshippers of the four virtues as much as they once did," The elder said.

"The Kingsclans don't appreciate us very much either," Promise said.

"Yes, I've heard. That's what we're here to help you with," laughed The Elder.

"I'm sorry to question you, but how are a group of worshippers going to help us win a war in any way, shape, or form?" Promise asked.

Samuel offered an answer. "What we've learnt in the past week or so we've spent with these men is that they have wandered all over Barbsav and have observant eyes that are keen for spotting people," he explained. "Over the next few weeks, they'll help us locate any of the former Clan Zhakkari warriors who escaped the battle like we did. A couple have already started the search."

"If they've been through what we have and survived, they'll want revenge on Osei. We won't even have to do much convincing. If we can locate them, they'll join our cause again, then we can start building our army," Ezekiel said. "A slow start, but a start nonetheless."

"We could also recruit some wandering warriors for you," The Elder said in addition. "I'm sure we'll find dozens and dozens of soldiers who can be persuaded to join your cause for a chance at glory in battle and a potential place of stay in your clan once you've rebuilt it."

"That would make for an even better start," Samuel chuckled.

Promise felt the trademark Zhakkari hope and ambition swirl through the air, bringing light to the stale cave.

"We're building our army," she said, as if she did not even believe herself when she spoke it aloud. "Are we actually going to do it? Are we genuinely going to start restoring our clan?"

"I believe so," Grace said with a sweet smile.

A GROWING CAUSE

SAMUEL Zhakkari was astonished by what was unfolding before him. Long weeks had come and gone since his and Ezekiel's reunion with their sisters, and the worshipping wanderers made good on their promises. The dry fields they relocated to were teeming with life. Many individuals ready to pursue the Zhakkari cause were scattered across one plain of uneven land.

Hours and hours of searching day in and day out had paid off to immense effect. The combined efforts of his siblings and the many wanderers resulted in up to one hundred good men populating the dark grasses in front of him and training with swords.

Rows of men with damaged, dirt-covered clothing and vexed expressions fought each other in simulated battles. Each hoped to unleash their bladed passion on the Kingsclans that destroyed their lands and forced them into Barbsav soon. The Zhakkari army was regrowing exponentially, soon to build momentum.

"We're building fast," Ezekiel commented as he came to his brother's side.

"I'm not sure we're building fast enough," Samuel said. "Will we be able to grow an army large enough to face the Kingsclans *before* they find out what we're planning?"

"This is the best we could hope for in that time frame," Ezekiel responded with a shrug. "We're already struggling to feed all these warriors, even with both our and the worship elder's cultivated food reserves, so the last thing we need is to be growing even quicker. Let's be grateful for how many men seem willing to fight with us."

"Right," Samuel accepted, lowering his head a touch.

He watched the men train. It seemed they were sustaining themselves on the passion of vengeance more than the food rations they had been given earlier.

"Have either of you seen Grace?" Promise asked. She was followed by a set of worshippers, the group marching across the field to meet with her brothers.

"I was told she was venturing on another recruit search with you," Samuel said.

"That was almost two days ago. Our search has long concluded," Promise said. "She left in the middle of it and told me she was heading back here, but I haven't seen her since," she explained.

"Neither have we," Samuel said.

"Perhaps she went on another recruiting search mission of her own?" Ezekiel asked.

"Perhaps," Promise muttered pensively.

The siblings saw the worship elder approach them with another set of companions following him. These men were in an uncharacteristically downbeat mood.

"What's the matter?" Samuel asked.

The Elder cleared his throat to speak. "Did you allow those barbarians to come here?" he asked.

The Elder pointed over the horizon to where another army was approaching their fields. Five groups of twenty Saxe-Barbarians trudged their way towards them, a sea of dark blue and grey debauchery.

The infamous Gideon Goldensight led the march, his eye trinket flashing as bright as his crooked smile.

"I didn't," Samuel grunted, displeased.

"I did," Ezekiel said.

Samuel faced his brother with incredulity. Ezekiel ignored him, standing straight as he waited for the barbarian leader to cross the field with the twenty men of his section.

A few of the Zhakkari warriors parted from the training field, wary of the barbarians that mingled amongst their ranks. Gideon Goldensight himself broke away from the ranks, addressing the Zhakkari siblings himself. Even Promise, who had not met him before, backed away from him with caution.

"Ezekiel Zhakkari. We meet again," Gideon greeted gleefully.

"Have you considered my offer?" Ezekiel asked.

"I have indeed."

"And what's your answer?"

Goldensight licked his teeth, delighting in the discomfort his smile was causing Ezekiel's siblings.

"My saxe-men and I will fight alongside you," Gideon answered. "We'll enjoy bringing a plague of swords to the Kingsclans of Civcaz."

"Good," Ezekiel grunted.

Samuel immediately dragged his older brother by the arm, pulling him aside for a talk. Gideon was left staring at Promise. The youngest Zhakkari was unwilling to even try and engage with him, walking away from them all.

"What in all souls do you think you're doing? Recruiting the man who made a sport out of hunting me?! Are you insane?" Samuel whispered furiously as he huddled by Ezekiel.

"Weren't you just saying you wished we could grow our army quicker?" Ezekiel asked.

"Weren't you the one who told me there are too many mouths to feed?" Samuel asked.

"We don't have to feed or train these men. They catch their own food and kill for fun. They're extra soldiers we can benefit from without having to waste extra resources," Ezekiel reasoned.

"Extra soldiers who are barbarians! I don't see how this is a moral or rational thing to do!" Samuel argued.

"We're not in a position where we can think of morals and rationality. It's not ideal, but I think we have to sacrifice a part of our souls now so that we can earn a larger portion once we've restored our clan," Ezekiel explained. "What they lack in justness and regality, they make up for in ingenuity and vitality. If we want to win this battle, we need to accommodate these Saxe-Barbarian fuckers for the time being. You know this."

Samuel glared at Goldensight. Gideon winked at him with his one eye. Samuel bit the inside of his mouth as he thought the Saxe-Barbarian offer through, drawing blood as he nervously chewed.

"How do we ensure their loyalty in battle? What do they gain in return?" Samuel asked.

"The chance to wreak havoc on Civcaz Hustans, maim and kill Kingsclan members, and steal all the gold they want without facing future repercussions for it after we win," Ezekiel explained.

On the training fields, the Saxe-Barbarians eagerly joined the sword-fighting drills. Some of them willingly let their opponents cut them out of pure enjoyment, a sight that made Samuel groan and sigh.

"Very well. If this is the best we can do, then so be it," Samuel accepted reluctantly.

Ezekiel left his brother's side to talk to Gideon Goldensight alone. Samuel shook his head as he watched the pair discuss.

***

When night fell, Promise refused to return to her sleeping quarters. The hundreds of newly-instated Zhakkari soldiers and Saxe-Barbarians slept in rows of camps with tents of cloth propped by spears and sleeping bags of sheep skin.

Promise stood awake. She stared out at the open field in front of her, not a muscle moved as she waited. After an hour, Samuel joined her side.

"Why are you still out here?" her brother asked.

"Grace is yet to return," Promise lamented.

"True," Samuel said.

He joined her in staring over the empty horizon of the endless field, also hoping Grace would emerge from the other side eventually. "Are you concerned?"

"Very," Promise sighed.

Samuel shook his head. "You shouldn't be. With all we've survived as of late, there's not a chance in any hell that Grace has hurt herself on a simple search mission," he assured her. "She's probably busy. I guarantee she'll be back here safe within the night, and if she's not, we'll go looking for and *find* her safe."

"Her safety's not my main point of concern," Promise sighed.

"It isn't?" Samuel asked. "Then what is?"

Promise swallowed a lump forming at the base of her throat. Samuel could see her fretting in her soft eyes. He could hear her internal monologue questioning whether she should reveal what she knew to him. Eventually, she did.

"A week or so before you and Ezekiel found us again, Jacqueline Bello came to our cave," Promise revealed with a worrisome gasp. "Apparently, the Bello family has convinced the Kingsclans to offer Grace a pardon, which she will be given if and only if she turns her back on us."

"Really?" Samuel asked.

"Really," Promise confirmed. "I'm worried she's travelling to their Hustan to discuss those terms."

Samuel's reaction was not quite what his sister was expecting. A blank, expressionless stare back. "Oh, I see," he said. "Do you think she *will* take the offer?"

Promise wiped her forehead. Just the thought of it stressed her out.

"I hope not," she said.

A JOINT VENTURE

GRACE Zhakkari felt alien sitting in the same place where she used to feel right at home. The comfortable, cushiony seats surrounding the gold-encrusted table felt stiff and wooden against her skin. She was in the dining room of the Clan Bello Hustan.

From the moment Grace had set foot on Bello land, from her giving of the coin to the merchant at the meat market to the long walk towards the Hustan gates on her lonesome, she had kept abreast of any signs of treachery. Though her arrival on Bello land might have indicated a belief that Jacqueline was being truthful with her offer, she kept a healthy suspicion of anything and everything.

She feared every person who passed her by, whether they be royal or peasant, for the slight chance they might capture or cut her and prove it all to be a trap. But no such thing had happened just yet. She had arrived at the Clan Bello Hustan safely.

Grace sat across the dining table from her former friend Jacqueline. The Bello daughter smiled with a forced gladness that did nothing to ease Grace's anxieties.

"It's so nice to have you here again. It truly is," Jacqueline beamed. Grace responded with a measured nod as the Bello daughter leaned over the empty table with tightly crossed arms.

"Where's the rest of your family? Aren't we supposed to prepare this pardon proposal?" Grace asked.

"My brother has important clan duties to attend to. Food and water distribution, that kind of boring stuff. But my parents will be with us shortly," Jacqueline said. "For now, why don't we just talk?"

Grace sighed, as unamused as a person could be. She slumped back in her chair.

"Once again, I'd like to apologise for the lies I told about you. I know it's a hard ask, but can you find it in your heart to forgive me?" Jacqueline asked.

"I suppose so," Grace said. "You convinced your family to give me the chance to be pardoned, so I can move past our grievances."

"Good. Good. It's the least I could have done to make up for my actions. Actions which I sorely, *sorely* regret," Jacqueline said.

Grace nodded awkwardly. The two women sat in silence for a few moments. Jacqueline's forced smile twitched slightly as Grace scanned the room for anything else to fix her eyes upon.

"Growing up, I used to want what you had," Jacqueline said, breaking the silence with conversation. "Your many talents, your effortless poise, the way people seemed to naturally love you. I was a little jealous, admittedly."

This was an understated truth, Grace thought, though she kept this comment to herself.

"But recently I realised it was stupid of me to be jealous. Do you know why, Grace?" Jacqueline asked.

Grace shook her head. "No. Tell me," she said, locking eyes with her once more.

"Because no matter how 'better' than me you were, I had more power. No matter how much my parents or my people loved you, it was *I* who was of an Arisclan, Bello, and you who were only of a Commonsclan, Zhakkari. Looking at it that way, it was stupid for me to have been so jealous of you, wasn't it?" Jacqueline laughed, her patronising giggles poisoning the air Grace breathed.

"Yeah, it was stupid," Grace laughed begrudgingly.

"At least we both realise it," Jacqueline chuckled. "Now we can focus on how we're going to use that power for both our benefits and get you that pardon you deserve."

"We can," Grace said, keeping any building resentment to a bare minimum.

A wrapping knock echoed from the other side of the golden dining room door. Jacqueline's eyes darted towards it with excitement.

"I think my parents have finally arrived," Jacqueline said, giving Grace a cheeky smile that was quickly yet weakly returned.

The Bello woman stepped out of her seat with grace and swanned over to the door.

With her back turned to Grace, a wicked smile imposed itself on her face. Her sunken eyes filled with malicious intent, unbeknownst to the Zhakkari at her table.

Jacqueline Bello had to force herself not to burst out into malicious cackles. She swung open the door.

"Defenders! Take this Zhakkari wench out-"
Jacqueline paused her spiteful demands as she saw the men who stood before her. She expected defenders to be at the door in place of her parents, in spite of having told Grace otherwise. She expected the defenders to be sporting

Arisclan Bello armour with the polished golden lioness crests. Instead, the defenders in front of her wore breastplates of welded linen layered with thick and black scabbard belts. This was the battle wear of Clan Zhakkari.

"What the fuck is this?!" Jacqueline furiously gasped, looking up and down at the baker's dozen of stationed Zhakkari warriors that cluttered her halls. She spun around to see the previously downtrodden Grace waltzing towards her with regained confidence.

"Why the sour attitude, friend? Hadn't you just called for defenders?" Grace mocked. "I bet you didn't expect them to be *my* defenders."

"How the fuck did you do this?!" Jacqueline seethed, grinding her teeth.

Grace waved to a figure behind the guards. A man revealed himself from out of the shadows of the hall. A tall man with a handsome face marred by disappointed anguish. Michel Bello pushed past the Zhakkari guards to stand by Grace's side. He looked upon his sister with shame.

"You, brother?! You helped her do this?!" Jacqueline cried in disbelief.

"Does that surprise you?" Michel said. "It shouldn't."

"These past few days you spent away, days you claimed you were sorting resources and reserves for our people, were spent helping this *whore* conspire against me?!" Jacqueline screamed in dismay. Dismay that Grace found incredibly amusing, more so than any joke she ever heard.

"You were conspiring against *her* with false pretences of proposals and pardons," Michel said.

"Which I'm insulted that you believed me gullible enough to fall for," Grace added.

"You were foolish enough to set foot on Bello land in the first place," Jacqueline scoffed.

"Not necessarily. You're forgetting I know this land quite well. I had my men sneak me here through a covered passageway in the forest before you even knew I was here. Then, I located your brother," Grace explained. "It was only then that I decided to take the risk and give the coin to the merchant, letting you know of my presence on the land. *Even then*, I still had a few defenders in hiding, ready to jump out if I didn't get to the Hustan safely. Once I did, and we were in this dining room, Michel just had to send away your defenders and let mine in."

Grace smiled, proud of her outmanoeuvring. Jacqueline's body shook with an intense energy she knew not what to do with other than quietly seethe. She looked back at her brother, Michel.

"And why should you care about whether I lured her back here on false pretences? She is a wrongdoer, coming from a family of even worse malefactors such as Samuel! She deserves any punishment that comes her way!" Jacqueline argued in a frothing tirade.

Michel shook his head in defiance. "Grace explained everything to me. From her brother's initial detainment to the battles and lies to Christian Osei's systematic dismantling of their clan," he said. "The Zhakkari's are guilty of nothing but defending themselves from Kingsclan Council injustice."

"You believe that?!" Jacqueline exclaimed.

"Yes," Michel said.

Grace's cheeks flushed with joy just from hearing that simple assertion.

Jacqueline grabbed him by the jewels around his neck.

"Michel, I am your sister! Your fucking *sister*!" she pleaded, half-angered, half-saddened. "Why would you side with her over me?!"

Michel pushed her off of him. "I always knew you were jealous of Grace. It was only natural. But your recent behaviour has shown me how corruptly envious and lacking in virtue you are!" he spat. "It sickens me to think that my sister was so *ill with envy* that she jumped at the chance to destroy the life of her longest friend and add to the lies of a conspiracy against her family that could have seen them killed! Truly sickening."

Jacqueline's lip quivered. She was speechless as she lost herself in her brother's judging gaze. "What about mother and father?! Are they fine with you doing this?!"

"I sent them on a trip to another land. They're taking a brief holiday until all the Zhakkari's issues have been resolved. But once they return, I'll tell them everything, and I'm sure they'll understand," Michel said.

Jacqueline winced. She could feel herself falling apart. Grace spoke. "Of all the things you told me at the cave that day, the *only* thing I believed was that your family still held love for me in their hearts," she said. "Who would've thought I'd be able to use their love to turn the tables on you and your *pathetic* attempts at trickery?"

The stern disparagement from her brother caused Jacqueline's crumbling facade of arrogance to shatter completely. The added comments from Grace had her drop to her knees.

"I hate you! I hate you both! I fucking hate you both!" Jacqueline screamed and cried. She pounded the floor beneath them as if in an effort to crack it open and have it swallow them whole. "Leave my Hustan! Leave my land! Fucking leave now!"

Grace laughed at the embarrassing display. "Alright, we'll leave," she said with a nonchalant shrug. "But we're taking your army with us."

Jacqueline looked up to Grace with tear-filled eyes of confusion. Grace chuckled down at her.

***

Samuel and Ezekiel trained alongside the Zhakkari warriors and Saxe-Barbarians on Barbsav fields as the evening's moonlight reflected off their blades. To Ezekiel's surprise and delight, Samuel had taken up the sword much more frequently and was showing great progress for a man as battle-shy as he was.

Promise stood a short walk away from them. For the past few days, they sent out some of the searching factions that were looking for recruits to keep an eye out for Grace, only to have never found her. Every evening, Promise would stand in that same position for hours. She would wait for Grace to return, wishing she would each day. That evening, she received her wish.

"Samuel! Ezekiel! Grace has returned!" Promise shouted. The pair of brothers dropped their swords as they rushed to her with haste.

"Where?" Samuel panted, out of breath from training. Promise pointed to a rapidly approaching swarm of men marching over the horizon. An armour-clad army hundreds strong. There were enough men there to replace the army they already had, Gideon Goldensight's barbarians included.

"And look at all the friends she brought with her," Ezekiel said.

The legion of men sported Civcaz helmets, battle gear, and weapons. They followed Grace's lead as she took them towards their Barbsav camp and training grounds.

The three siblings marvelled as they watched the new army of men join the ranks of warriors and barbarians as seamlessly as if they had always trained there.

"Excuse my absence. I was quite busy," Grace said. She walked to her siblings with both hands clasped together in as prideful a manner as the lion emblems on the armours of the warriors she brought.

"Are those Arisclan Bello warriors?!" Samuel asked, his voice cracking with dubious shock. He noticed the emblems on every single one of their new forces. Grace nodded.

"And they're here to fight for us?" Promise asked.

"They are," Grace answered.

"How did you convince Bello warriors to fight alongside us?!" Ezekiel asked, grinning from ear to ear.

"I had to convince Michel first. I took a risk and assumed he still loved me enough to believe my explanations for everything that had happened to us. Thankfully, he did. Then, I outsmarted Jacqueline and exposed her efforts to try and trick me into accepting the fake pardon, which further convinced him to join our cause against the Kingsclans," Grace explained to her siblings. "So now, Jacqueline's in detainment, and the Clan Bello army is ours."

The deepest sigh of relief escaped Promise's mouth involuntarily. "*That's* why you wanted to visit the Clan Bello Hustan."

"It was," said Grace. "I know what the rest of you are thinking. It *was* a very dangerous plan where I had to take a lot of serious risks. But look at what I achieved! Now we-"

Promise interrupted her sister in the warmest way possible as she pulled her in for a hug. "I'm so sorry I doubted you."

Grace enveloped herself in the warmth as she hugged her sister. Tears from Promise's eyes dropped delicately onto her shoulder.

"It's alright, I forgive you," Grace laughed as the two broke off the hug whilst still holding each other's arms.

Samuel stretched his hands out in a glorious gesture as he counted the hundreds of men who had gathered in their field to train with the sword.

"We have *more* than enough fighters for Osei and Khoza," he laughed.

"We do," agreed Ezekiel, licking his lips at the thought of tasting battle.

It would not be long until the Zhakkari siblings returned to Civcaz with their army. Soon, they would challenge the Kingsclans to take back what was theirs.

A JUST FIGHT

PROMISE Zhakkari was ill at ease. Through even the most intense forces of effort, she could not keep herself still.

She moved constantly, readjusting her position as she sat on the cape-buffalo-fur carpet that covered the floors. She counted the markings on the wall, the crude depictions of swords and lions carved into white marble, over and over until it gave her a headache. Nothing she did could put her mind at rest. Not when she knew what was happening a few miles away.

"Worried?" one of the worship wanderers who sat next to her asked.

"Naturally," Promise sighed.

She was accompanied by elderly worship wanderers, sick warriors, and the women and children of those who fought for the Zhakkari cause in an abandoned stronghold.

Promise chose to stay with all the vulnerable members of their factions. She and these vulnerable folk were safe within the confines of the abandoned war quarters. A legion of defenders protected them as her siblings took an army straight to Civcaz's mainland.

"Your siblings are intelligent and brave warriors who are leading battle-hardened men and being spurred on by the support of righteous, virtuous people such as you and me. There is no reason for you to be worried," the worship wanderer assured her.

"I'll keep that in mind," Promise sighed.

A new set of worship wanderers entered the stronghold, joined by warriors that Promise did not recognise as being of the Zhakkari, Saxe, or Bello faction. One of these warriors was swaddling a baby wrapped in cloth.

"The leaders of Arisclan Irie answered the contact. They came by just now," a worship wanderer said as he walked alongside the baby-carrying warrior.

"Are they outside?" Promise asked.

"No. They didn't stop by. They said they didn't want to see you but needed to give you what's yours."

"What? What does that even mean?"

"Your child, Promise. You're being reunited with your child," they revealed.

Promise's heart beat with rapid anticipation as she saw the man bring the baby to her. "Are you serious?" she gasped. The man nodded.

Whether her former parents-in-law wanted to see her face or not was of the least concern to her. She felt as if her soul was as light as air, light enough to float over all the lands as her sweet baby boy was softly handed to her.

"My sweet Joseph," Promise gushed, softly brushing a finger against his cheek.

The people of the stronghold formed a circle around her, watching on with smiles as sweet as his. The Zhakkari baby giggled and cooed.

The sensation of her Joseph being in her hands again was enough to quell Promise's woes. Within an instant, her faith in her sibling's battle success doubled.

They had no choice but to succeed, she reasoned. They must for the future of her baby boy and every child of Clan Zhakkari.

***

Christian Osei enjoyed his wife's embrace from behind as she caressed his head. The couple savoured silence together within a pool room. Of all the rooms in the Clan Osei Hustan, being in this one put the Kingsclan leader's mind at ease the most. A room scarcely lit but for one shining light emerging from a hole in the ceiling.

The light beamed upon a pool of green water surrounded by stone barriers. Christian Osei and his devoted wife, Florence, bathed in the pool. Christian's eyes closed as his wife trickled her fingers across his face with one hand and trickled soothing waters down his back with the other.

"You're always so stressed, my dear," she said.

"All of Civcaz relies on my rule," Christian sighed. "I have every reason to be stressed."

"Then I have every reason to wash your stress away," Florence smirked.

Christian breathed softly out of his nose, enjoying the warm waters his wife dripped on his neck.

Blood-curdling screams disrupted the Osei couple's peace. The room shook slightly, the pool's waters jolting as bewilderment marked both their faces. The heavy stone door to their sanctuary was beaten upon with desperate fists until it was broken down.

A Clan Osei warrior stumbled over the pool barrier, landing before the couple. Florence gasped at the deep scars

174

covering the man's face. Pieces of armour chipped off of him, joining his blood in rusting the water to contamination.

"What fucking possessed you to disturb my wife and I in such a *dastardly* state?!" Christian cursed at the man.

"The Zhakkari's are back," the Kingsclan warrior croaked through a mouth full of blood.

Christian froze as his wife gripped his chest with concern. Surprise, anger, fear, and a lust for violence all fought for supremacy, each vying for a place in his heart and soul as his face grew colourless.

No one emotion was able to beat out the other. They combined to fuel a purposeful march out of the room.

Christian Osei headed towards his stratagem-quarters to retrieve his armour and blades.

***

Christian exited the front gates of his clan's Hustan wearing emerald gems on a suit of armour that shone brighter than the moon's light. He walked down a levered drawbridge as twenty other Kingsclan warriors trailed behind him. The vast open meadows that surrounded the most isolated and pristine part of Civcaz land were being profaned by the trawls of war. Blue wildflowers painted red with spilt blood.

Christian assessed the boundless battlefield that had been made before him. As far as he could remember, the Zhakkari army did not have enough men to challenge the Osei army on its lonesome, and that was before he had utterly destroyed their clan and ruined their land. But now they were. The Zhakkaris should not have been able to build a large enough army to even breach the land, never mind cut through his meadows. Yet he saw his forces in a violent struggle against an army of men that exceeded theirs. Even with the approaching Clan Khoza reinforcements to supplement his numbers, the Zhakkari forces were still more than enough to match the Kingsclans.

Christian Osei saw men of different creeds amongst his opponents. Clan Bello men, Clan Irie men, Wandering Warriors of Barbsav, and Saxe-Barbarians. All of these factions banded together to fight for the damned family he had set to destroy.

Osei had no time to brood in the anger that filled him whole. A selection of Zhakkari warriors charged towards him, their weapons raised and eyes full of hate. He and his Kingsclan men prepared to engage in immediate conflict.

"Fucking traitors. All of them," Christian Osei grunted as he unsheathed his sword. "Zhakkari-apologist scum!"

He screamed, running onward with the desire to kill everything in his path.

***

Samuel was not a fighter. His father knew this when he trained him, his mother knew this when she observed his training, and he knew it every time he picked up a blade. It was why he focused all of his energy growing up on becoming an ingenious scholar and polymath. It was why Ezekiel chastised him for being unfit during their mock battles. It was why the other children saw him as an easy victim during his schooling.

But Samuel sought to fight on the battlefield regardless. Weeks of intense training in combination with a fervid passion for his clan and his people emboldened him enough to involve himself in the battles on the Kingsclan meadows. Like any other warrior would.

Samuel moved with roving squads of warriors, in which their faction's key task was to send the unified armies of Osei and Khoza into disarray. Their individual tasks were simpler. They were to deal quick and efficient blows to the enemy and force them to split into smaller groups of warriors to pick off.

Samuel and a series of excited Saxe-Barbarians utilised their knives, smallswords, and daggers to methodically isolate the strongest and largest Kingsclan warriors with sneak attacks and slash-and-run executions.

Samuel sprinted behind a Clan Osei warrior battling a Clan Bello warrior. With a smooth, dragging motion, he cut across the nape of the Osei warrior's neck, killing him. He kept his momentum, sprinting powerfully as he located his next Kingsclan victim.

For the first time in his life, Samuel felt an abundance of vitality enrich his soul.

A REGAL WAR

GRACE Zhakkari stood upon a cliff overlooking the *War of the Osei Meadows*. She and her team of archers stationed there rained arrows on the Osei and Khoza men on a rocky hill below them. The pierced bodies fell into the river stream that cut through the land. The second Zhakkari child stood with purpose. She elegantly reached into the quiver on her back for arrows, placed them in her bow, and launched them towards Kingsclan warrior hearts.

Stationed behind her team were another team of archers. The team were lined across them in a protective stance, creating a barrier between Grace's team on the cliff and the forests behind them. This was a cautionary measure to prevent any Kingsclan forces from attacking the archers and forcing them to give up their vantage point, as well as a simple system that allowed Grace and her comrades to continue with their aid from the sky. Their precise arrows hit their targets from an elevated position from which they could not be struck back.

Grace paused for a moment to observe the battlefield. She assessed Samuel's battle tactics on full display.

Grace could see him and his roving squad of Zhakkari warriors and Saxe-Barbarians scattering the Kingsclan warriors with their swift cuts and endless rushes. She could also see other strategies and plans that Samuel had detailed beforehand play out in different sections of the meadows.

Further squads of archers speckled across the fighting engaged in the cruel yet efficient practice of shooting arrows into the eyes of Kingsclan lions, preventing their enemies from performing cavalry charges or from even mounting them in the first place.

On the other hand, their side utilised their lions in a manner considered unorthodox to traditional Civcaz warfare. Ferocious felines trained to attack upon the scent of Kingsclan-quality gems were released from the forests and over the hills. These bloodthirsty cats wet their fangs as they sank them into Osei and Khoza armour, gnawing at the Kingsclan warriors and separating all of their limbs from all of their bodies.

The roving squads of warriors dealing cut-and-run blows were slowing down, losing their momentum. Groups of Kingsclan warriors saw this as a chance to rid themselves of the pestering squad, pouncing on them at once.

This, however, proved to be another tactic of Samuel's making. As soon as they did so, lines of warriors flanked them from either side, finally engaging in direct conflict with an overwhelming assault. Grace aided this frontal assault. She fired arrows in rapid succession, piercing through the heads of their enemy.

As Grace reached for her bow to fire her thirtieth arrow, she found her quiver to be empty.

"I need more arrows!" Grace shouted to the men of the defensive archer squad who lined the forest.

One of the men turned to her. "I'll retrieve some from the hidden stock," he said as she marched over to him.

The man handed Grace his bow and quiver, picking out a sword from a muddy crevice in the ground to replace it. Another one of these archers followed in his footsteps, taking out an axe.

The two of them ventured into the forests in search of the supplies. Grace left her post at the cliff, filling in for the two archers who had left their positions on the line.

As she joined the defensive line, she caught wind of a series of Khoza soldiers attempting to blindside them by climbing a rocky hill west of their position.

Grace dropped her bow and arrow for a moment and attended to the same crevice in the ground where the archers had kept their bladed weapons. She searched underneath the blades until she found a metal container. The same metal container that held that awful liquid substance that Promise had concocted using Samuel's notes.

Grace opened the container very carefully. She took one of her arrows and dipped the bladed point into the vile purple liquid. A fresh batch had been made, with tens of these containers being Promise's contribution to the war effort. The liquid corroded the metal on the arrow to a certain extent, only just about keeping the bladed point sharp. The perfect battle enhancer.

She fired the poisoned arrow at a Khoza warrior who climbed the hill. The arrow struck him in the stomach, starting the gradual process of a painful death. Its corrosive properties burned a hole through his stomach faster than the blood could leave it.

Just this one strike was enough to dampen Khoza morale. The sight of their fallen comrade, a warrior whose stomach continued to degrade and peel away after his death, was enough to prompt a retreat.

Grace grunted, carefully dipping more arrows in the substance as she prepared to finish off the Khoza hill-climbers.

***

William of Kingsclan Khoza's stuffy disposition often had those who faced him on the battlefield surprised beyond comprehension. The fact that a man as stodgy as he was proved to be such a formidable fighter was astonishing to most who heard of his battles, never mind seen them.

William Khoza thought himself to be fighting for the honour of the Khoza people, the Kingsclans, Christian Osei, and Civcaz itself. Thus, every swing of his sword was completed with fervent passion.

He drove his sword through the stomach of a Zhakkari warrior whose armour plate he had previously destroyed. A Saxe-Barbarian came barrelling towards him wildly, to which he scoffed. He dispatched the unruly fighter with a quick, effortless drive of the sword in and out of the top of his chest. He killed the next man who dared to face him, knocking the helmet from his head with a mocking smack from the end of his sword, then thrusting the blade through.

He saw another soldier of the Zhakkari forces attempt to flee battle, the man realising that he was outmatched and would meet the same fate as the last. Khoza would allow no such cowardice in his regal presence. He butchered the man's back, cleaving his sword down the space between his shoulder blades and along his spine.

William had destroyed all enemy warriors close to his position. The Khoza clan leader searched the general area for another enemy to slice into. He found the perfect target.

"Samuel," Khoza scoffed.

The third Zhakkari child stood ten paces away from him on the flowery battlefield. He held a two-pronged traditional Zhakkari dagger.

"William," Samuel scoffed back.

"Your clan seems to be causing us a lot of trouble," Khoza said, gesturing at the bloody meadows surrounding them. "I don't feel bad for all we've done to you."

Samuel laughed. "What I'd like to know is why you even ushered me onto the Shared Council in the first place. Especially if you always planned to do *all you've done*."

"I needed to assess you. From what I recall from our days of schooling together as children, you were quite intelligent. I thought to myself, *perhaps he might have something to offer*," William explained. "I thought wrong."

"You weren't wrong. I would have done great things for the council," Samuel said.

"I doubt that. I regretted giving you a seat the second you spoke during your first meeting. Hearing what came out of your mouth, it's no wonder the other children tortured you growing up," Khoza scorned. "I think I'll reconnect with some of them shortly. They'll be amused to hear of how I cut through you."

"Come and try," Samuel goaded.

William did exactly that. He closed the distance between the two of them, the Khoza family sword whistling as it sliced through the air in Samuel's direction.

Samuel's training with Ezekiel seemed to pay off. He was able to dodge the constant strikes from the Khoza longsword. But that was all he could do. William Khoza was far too skilled in comparison to him. Any attempt Samuel made to strike back was deflected faster than he could think to send another.

Samuel continued to dodge and back away, unable to find an opening for attack. He avoided a huge sweeping blow, ducking underneath Khoza's sword time after time.

Though he found himself out of the sword's cutting path, he lost his footing, falling to the ground. His Kingsclan rival laughed at his lack of coordination.

"Weak of mind, weak of body," Khoza mocked. The fight had just begun, yet he thought it already done. He was ready to deliver a killing blow to his childhood enemy. Samuel Zhakkari's head was to be split in two.

At least it would have been, had it not been for an unlikely intervention.

William Khoza had neither the time nor the reflexes to avoid an attack that blindsided him at a moment's notice. A Saxe-Man rushed to Khoza and sank a knife in his side. The Shared Council member looked down in shock as he saw the most notorious of the barbarians twist the blade.

"Kingsclan blood," Gideon Goldensight mocked, licking his lips.

Goldensight poked a finger into Khoza's wound and brought it to his face, painting the blood around his mouth.

"Dirty degenerate barbarian fuck!" William Khoza screamed. He kicked the Saxe-Barbarian leader to the ground, ignoring the stinging pain of the knife being yanked out of him in the process.

William reached for his sword on the floor, only to stumble. A searing pain developed at the back of his neck, a pain so great it robbed him of the strength to even scream in agony. The Khoza clan leader turned back to Samuel. He saw that he was in possession of the red-soaked blade that had dealt the awful cut.

"Farewell," Samuel chuckled. He slid the dagger across his rival's Adam's apple.

William Khoza fell. He choked on his blood, cursing incomprehensibly as he succumbed to a shameful death at the hands of a Zhakkari.

A VITAL BATTLE

EZEKIEL Zhakkari had been in many battles, though this was the first one where he fought with caution.

With his last battle against Kingsclan forces still fresh in his mind, the horrible wounds that were inflicted on him that day stung. It was almost as if they were being reopened by the memories alone.

Ezekiel learnt from his mistakes on the battlefield this time around. He fought the war in the Osei meadows with tact, killing his enemies with suave skill as opposed to the brute force that was natural to him.

A deft manoeuvre saw Ezekiel able to parry a Khoza warrior's sword with such finesse that the blade slipped out of the fighter's grip. Ezekiel finished the exposed warrior with a signature battle-axe slash to the chest.

The plentiful faction of fellow warriors who joined him in battle cheered as that warrior's death meant a complete and utter clearing of that section of the battlefield.

Ezekiel glanced over the dead-body-embellished meadow. At that stage in the battle, most of the Khoza forces had either been destroyed or forced to retreat. He even heard that their leader, William Khoza, had been killed on the other side of the battlefield by none other than his brother, Samuel. An impressive feat that would make any older brother proud.

The Khoza front was finished. To make matters worse for the Kingsclan side, the Osei army was on its last legs.

Ezekiel's men started to rest, becoming complacent. They gave their tired bodies a break, seeing as the battles were soon to end.

***

Kingsclan reinforcements came in the form of fifty Arisclan Rashid soldiers. A small force in terms of replacing the numbers that the Oseis and Khozas had already lost, but enough men to prevent the Zhakkari armies from pressing forward for a Hustan-seizing victory.

Warriors of the land's most battle-ready clan dismounted their lions. Ezekiel cut his rest short to confront the fresh army. His men begrudgingly charged after him.

"We've already fucked the Khoza forces into the dirt!" Ezekiel roared gloriously as they closed the gap between them and the Rashids. "Let's fuck these also!"

"Yeah!" his men roared with him, pursuing further glory in blood.

The two armies clashed with one another in a mixed sea of Zhakkari black and Rashid maroon. The dozenth gruesome battle of the day was well underway.

Ezekiel delivered many killing blows within the first few minutes of the clash. He mowed down the reinforcements with measured onslaughts of aggression, blitzing axe swipes and piercing daggers, cutting Rashid warrior flesh and bones.

He exited the fray, pausing his axe assaults and scanning his surroundings. He searched the field for one specific Rashid warrior. A face he had not seen in a long time but had not forgotten.

"Are you looking for me, Ezekiel?" Ibrahim Rashid chuckled.

Ezekiel witnessed his handsome yet smarmy face once again, chuckling away. Ezekiel grunted, already tired of his faux-affable mockery.

"I hope you're not upset about me imprisoning you in a hole. Father's orders, remember?" Ibrahim giggled.

Ezekiel pointed his axe at his former brother-in-arms.

"Remember our little tournament bout?" he asked.

"Unfortunately," Ibrahim snickered.

"You and I are going to fight again, and I'm going to win *again*," Ezekiel asserted. "Only this time, you won't be able to run back to your father like a lapdog. He's going to learn what it means to outlive one's offspring."

Ibrahim laughed. "I said it before, and I'll say it again: must everything be a fight with you? Can't you just do as you're told?" he asked mockingly.

"How fucking spineless can you be?" Ezekiel asked. "I'm going to enjoy cutting you to pieces."

"If you want a fight, very well. But don't be surprised if this ends up being your last," Ibrahim said.

Ezekiel and Ibrahim's ears suffered the simultaneous sharp ringing of blade slamming against blade with powerful might. Both of them had attempted to land the first strike and had failed to surprise the other.

The two warriors broke into a mirrored dance of potentially killing hits, deflecting each other's blades.

Both were determined to crown themselves the unequivocal winner of their final spar.

***

Christian Osei pulled his sword out of the stomach of a Zhakkari warrior victim, spilling his guts and entrails over a bundle of indigenous flowers. With his gruelling bout concluded, he assessed how his men were faring.

The Khoza men were nowhere to be seen, the Clan Rashid reinforcements were slowly being overwhelmed, and most concerningly, his Osei forces had been pushed so far back into submission that if he turned, he could see the gates of his Hustan.

"This cannot happen. This must not happen," he muttered. Only a few dozen men stood between him and a large assembly of Zhakkari warriors who would cut through them in no time.

Christian Osei clenched his jaw. He tensed the muscles in his body, attempting to dispel the fear that was seeping through them. It was no use. He abandoned the last of his men who fought valiantly in defence of his Hustan.

The Kingsclan leader disappeared, running towards the Hustan he was supposed to be helping to protect.

The most powerful man in Civcaz was willing to be seen dashing away from battle with his tail in between his legs if it meant preserving himself within the safe walls of his castle abode.

***

Ezekiel's muscles tired fast. His constant ongoing duel with Ibrahim was proving to be the greatest Zhakkari warrior's longest and hardest bout.

No amount of focus and skill was sharp enough on his part to land a clean blow on the eldest Rashid son. The linen on his armour was down to its last layer, worn and torn from the day's constant warring.

Ezekiel recalled his late father Kinglsey's training in his youth. He decided the best defence was offence, stopping his deflecting parries and lunging forward for a bolder attack than his previous.

Ezekiel levied a powerful swing of his axe, a style of blow fast enough to cut most men before they could even realise what happened. Ibrahim was not like most men, evading the axe's curved blade.

"Far too slow," Ibrahim laughed, retaliating with a quick swipe of his shortsword.

The blade sliced through the final layer of linen on Ezekiel's destroyed armour and met his chest. Ezekiel felt blood drip down him in profuse waves, his healed wounds opening up again. A mountain of pain descended upon him, weakening him at the knees and delighting Ibrahim.

Ezekiel performed another bold axe swing. Ibrahim stopped him with a slam of the hilt of his sword, a blunt attack damaging his nose and bursting his mouth.

Both of Ezekiel's orifices were filled with the taste and smell of dirty copper. His head rang whilst his ears were plagued by Ibrahim's irritating laughs.

"Not exactly like our last fight, is it?" Ibrahim chuckled. Ezekiel felt ill from both Ibrahim's blows and how sick he was of the Rashid's incessant laughter. He vowed to himself at that moment that this would be the last time he would ever suffer hearing it.

As Ibrahim lunged forward to attack him, he drew mucus from the deepest depths of his injured throat. In a crass jolt forward, Ezekiel spat bloody phlegm into his former battle-mate's left eye.

"What the fuck was that?!" Ibrahim yelped in disgust. As he wiped the spit, Ezekiel picked up his axe and sliced a wound across his left ankle.

"Fuck!" Ibrahim cried out.

The Rashid man groaned, now being the one weak at the knees as his body tilted to the right side. Ezekiel balanced him out, cutting him down by his left ankle. The Rashid warrior screamed with shocked horror as he fell, barely processing the quick, gruesome succession of events.

Ibrahim gasped as he tried to prop himself up. Ezekiel shoved the Arisclan warrior's own sword through his chest, pinning him to the ground.

Ibrahim Rashid lay on the meadow's flowers, dying. His eyes widened as Ezekiel approached him. He was yet to comprehend how he had been defeated. His fading mind could not register that he failed to crown himself the victor of his last ever battle.

As he looked up to the Zhakkari standing over his leaking body, his loss settled in. Ezekiel was no stranger to standing over the dying bodies of other warriors and the looks of despair they would give him before they passed on. To his surprise, Ibrahim accepted it well. He stared up at him with a blood-soaked smile.

"You win again, friend," Ibrahim laughed.

With his last portion of strength and surprising speed, he unsheathed a knife from his scabbard and plunged it into his heart. Ibrahim smiled one last time as he died, having robbed the Zhakkari of the satisfaction that would have come with landing the killing blow.

"Cunt," Ezekiel grunted.

He left his former friend's corpse, looking to rejoin the rest of his Zhakkari men.

He saw the last of the Rashid reinforcements being taken down, a dozen of Ibrahim's comrades struggling against the superior Zhakkari force. Those few Arisclan warriors were the last enemies present on the battlefield.

Ezekiel's slim, piercing eyes zoned in on the gates of Kingsclan Osei. Zhakkari men were storming the Hustan.

All that was left to do was capture the Kingsclan Hustan for a complete Zhakkari victory.

AN INGENIOUS REVELATION

SAMUEL Zhakkari watched in intrigue as the Zhakkari, Saxe, Bello, and Irie men of his army stormed the gates of the defenceless Clan Osei Hustan. His weeks spent planning this ambush yielded the most positive results. He and his siblings' valiant efforts in battle achieved their clan's greatest success. The Zhakkari front was forcing itself into the Hustan of the most powerful Kingsclan in the land, minutes away from complete domination.

"Where's Ezekiel?" Grace asked as she ran towards him. She left her battles unscathed but for a small scar on her face and two small acidic burn marks on her arms.

"I think he ran in there with the rest," Samuel said, gesturing towards the Osei Hustan at the end of the meadow.

"Let's join him then," Grace said.

She left her brother to join the Zhakkari men rushing through to the gates. Samuel smiled and followed suit.

***

Christian Osei shielded himself within the stone confines of his Hustan's pool room. Like the man who had warned him of the Zhakkari's arrival, his blood and rusted armour dirtied the waters as he waded in darkness and defeat.

The sounds of grief echoed through the walls of his Hustan as he heard his men lose further sections of it to Zhakkari forces. He could hear the wily screams of Saxe-Barbarians most of all, in combination with the jingles and clangs of his gold being pillaged by them.

The strongest leader in all of Civcaz had been dealt a devastating loss, one from which he knew he would never recover. He sat in his dirty pool water, waiting for death to arrive. It soon came.

The stone door to his pool room burst down. Death arrived in the shape of three disgruntled siblings. A blood-lusted Ezekiel Zhakkari, a stern-faced Grace Zhakkari, and the one whose presence bothered him the most, a smug-looking Samuel Zhakkari.

"Look at you. A family coming to take my head together," Christian Osei angrily mocked. "Be done with it already! Come! Come take my head!"

Samuel raised his eyebrows at Christian. "I like this Hustan. I think we'll take it as our own," he commented as he looked around the intricate patterns painted over the walls that were scarcely visible due to the dim light that shone through a hole in the ceiling.

"It'll be a good replacement for ours, seeing as you burnt it down and tore it brick by brick," Ezekiel said, smiling malevolently.

"A very good replacement," Grace added with amusement.

Christian Osei grunted. "What is the fucking meaning of this?" he complained. "Cease your taunting! If you're planning on killing me, just fucking kill me!"

"We'll kill you in due time. We need an explanation first," Samuel said.

"An explanation for what?" Christian asked.

"For why you and the Kingsclan Council did everything you did to our family?" Grace reminded him.

"You're going to kill me whether I explain or not. Why should I give you that satisfaction?" Christian scoffed.

Ezekiel stepped forward with menace. "Because if you don't tell us, we *won't* kill you. We'll cut off all your limbs as well as your penis. We'll keep you alive and torture you in your own Hustan dungeons for months."

Christian Osei assessed the three siblings. In spite of his mocking smile, he knew they were serious. Samuel grabbed the Kingsclan leader by the broken jewel necklaces that decorated his destroyed armour.

"Why did you frame me for those crimes? Why did you mar my family with conspiracies?" Samuel asked. "Why were you so hellbent on the destruction of Clan Zhakkari?"

Christian Osei sighed, accepting his hopeless defeat. He cleared his throat and told all.

"Remember Clan Godwin? The *former* most powerful Kingsclan in all the land?"

"I remember how you and the other Kingsclan members destroyed them completely and tortured their members," Samuel answered.

"Well, there's a reason we did. They were too powerful for their own good, and my clan didn't like that. Not one bit," Christian explained. "I'm not sure if any of you are old enough to remember, but my clan wasn't always one of the most powerful. We rose from grief to glory after my father found a diamond reserve on the land under our meadows. Growing up, I saw my family rise from a lowly Commonsclan all the way to a Kingsclan that stood above the rest. Riches and raw power were thrust upon us. But there was one clan we could never seem to rise above, no matter how much money and power we accumulated. One clan that seemed to always be ahead of us. The founders of the Land of Civcaz. Fucking Kingsclan Godwin."

The siblings huddled around Osei, crouching down and listening as if he were an elderly relative telling them a tale.

"Our clan planned to take them down so that we could reign supreme. My father, Adam Osei, was the one who started the slow and gradual process. Over the years, we spread rumours, disparaging tidings of the Godwins and their character as a clan. We took their tales of being brave conquerors who gloriously ruled over the Civcaz lands as its strongest enforcers and perverted them. We twisted them until they started to sound like tales of an oppressive force of unjust, unruly leaders," Christian Osei continued. "That's where the Kingsclan Shared Council came in. There was another slow, methodical process going on over the years. One in which a council of sycophants was formed, people who listened to every word my father said. By the time I came of age, the Shared Council was filled with influential figures who treated *my* word as God's, like that foolish William Khoza. I used that power to double my father's efforts until Clan Godwin's good name was completely sullied. Once we had convinced the people of Civcaz that the Godwins were no good, it justified our building campaigns of physical attacks on them to match the verbal. We stamped out Kingsclan Godwin until they were nothing more than the people of the land's torture victims."

"I always knew that the treatment of the Godwins was somehow unjust," Samuel said, shaking his head in disapproval.

"I'm failing to see what this has to do with your attempts to stamp *us* out," Grace said.

Christian tilted his head back, dipping it in water as he rested against a rock ledge. "Have you noticed how much Civcaz society has degraded as a whole?" he asked, diverting from his original story.

"What?" Grace asked.

"Broken families are becoming the norm. There are drunken mothers, absent fathers, and neglected children everywhere. Young girls abandon their schooling to become pleasure-maidens. Young boys spend their time drinking in taverns rather than swinging swords in training yards. Saxe-Barbarians live amongst high clans and turn their villages inside out. Temples are being torn down, and their worshippers are prevented from acquiring land to live on. Last but not least, general violence and disorder are a lot more common," Christian listed.

"Is this relevant to your explanation?" Ezekiel scoffed.

"It's very relevant," Christian laughed.

"We *have* noticed how much Civcaz society has degenerated," Samuel answered impatiently. "I'm assuming you're responsible?"

Christian nodded. "Your assumptions are correct. Over the past few years, I've been intentionally implementing policies that work to cripple the land and its people."

"And why in all virtues have you been doing that?" Samuel asked.

Christian rolled his eyes. "That should be obvious to someone as *supposedly* smart as you, Samuel," he sighed. "The weaker a nation, the easier it is to control. The easier people are to control, the smoother your reign as ruler."

An acute pain formed in the middle of Samuel's head as he bemusedly glared at Christian Osei and his candid rants.

The Zhakkari put everything together, his mind spinning as he figured out the reason behind the Kingsclan Council's attack on their family. Before he could speak out about these revelations, Osei did it for him.

"Though I paid little attention to you myself, I'd heard a little about you Zhakkaris from Khoza. A Commonsclan of four siblings that was quickly scaling the ladders of power in Civcaz. The sister who had married into Arisclan Irie. The brother who fought in the brave armies of Arisclan Rashid. The sister who was adored by the people of Arisclan Bello. And most of all, the strange, clever brother he knew from his childhood, who had done much to help the people of his land. A boy who wanted to continue his work on a grander scale by securing a seat on the Kingsclan Council," Christian continued. "Khoza warned me that if I let you rise, you'd be another Clan Godwin in the making. He warned that you'd become a powerful thorn in our sides that needed to be plucked. But I wanted to vet you first, so I told him to bring you to the first Kingsclan meeting."

"I remember that meeting like it was yesterday. You and your lackeys made it seem like I was a fool for bringing up my proposals," Samuel recalled.

"As soon as you started talking about implementing policies that would firmly set the four virtues into the souls of the people of Civcaz, I knew you were a threat to my plans. I knew you and your family of ambitious strivers, desperate to act above your station, needed to have your names ruined and power dulled."

"And that's why you attacked us so thoroughly," Samuel stated.

A deranged smile occupied Christian's face as he locked eyes with him. "Yes. That's why I performed a similar campaign with you Zhakkaris to the one I used to crush the Godwins, only fast-tracked, and intertwined with my other plans," Osei said. "But I realise that was a mistake. I underestimated your capabilities. I underestimated your irritating insistence on fighting until the bitter end."

"You did," Ezekiel agreed sternly.

"I shouldn't have kept you alive as a vanquished foe whose presence struck fear in the people of Civcaz's hearts. I shouldn't have wasted my time with all that. Killing you with no fanfare would've sufficed," Osei snarled. "I should have ended your bloodline entirely."

"There's no point in concerning yourself with past regrets," Grace said. "You're the one whose bloodline is about to be ended."

Christian Osei's half-furious, mischievous smirk wiped off his face as the reality of his situation set in for the final time. Each of the three Zhakkari siblings unsheathed their blades and closed him in. Together, they performed an empire-ending simultaneous attack.

Time slowed down from Christian's perspective as he powerlessly watched Grace's tightly gripped arrow, Ezekiel's axe, and Samuel's dagger fly towards his body.

The Kingsclan leader was in delirious denial. Even as the blades hacked at his meat and sprayed blood into the air, his mind did not want to admit that this was the end of him, that his body was dying, and that he was soon to be no more. He lay there, refusing to register the excruciatingly torturous pain he was going through as the Zhakkari siblings sank blade after blade into his bruised flesh.

A final strike from Samuel ended the Osei reign for good. The traditional two-pronged Zhakkari dagger was firmly driven through Christian's skull.

***

Promise rode in one carriage of a series of lion-drawn vehicles approaching the Osei Meadows. With the worship wanderers and other vulnerable members of the stronghold riding alongside her, they arrived at the Hustan's gates.

Promise saw her three siblings waiting for them there with prideful smiles. Her heart swelled with joyous relief. A Zhakkari victory had been secured.

"They did it!" the Elder celebrated.

"You did it!" Promise cheered.

"We did it," Samuel confirmed. "Clan Zhakkari will finally be restored."

A DIFFERENT TOMORROW

CIVCAZ, as an ancient land, was still recovering from the tumultuous events it had been subjected to during Clan Osei's reign and the Kingsclan struggle against the Zhakkari's.

A year had passed since that struggle's conclusion. There were still blood-stained roads, destroyed villages, and affected food supplies. Despite all these prevalent issues, those who ruled the lands felt hopeful for the future.

Samuel Zhakkari stood on the balcony of the former Osei Hustan, now known as the Zhakkari Hustan. He looked down upon the flowery blue meadows that were now the property of his family and people. A family and people who had been promoted from the lowly, infamous Commonsclan Zhakkari to the esteemed Kingsclan Zhakkari.

Samuel enjoyed seeing his people celebrate the very essence of life together in the meadows. He adored observing the festivities of Zhakkari folk on that sweltering summer day, paying special attention to his siblings.

He saw Promise with her baby, Joseph, mingling with a man and his daughter of a similar age to her son. He was a tall, graceful, and exceptionally handsome man who, like

Promise, had the misfortune of losing his spouse and becoming a single parent. From what Samuel had heard, she was considering remarrying, and he was her first choice. If the wedding was to be anything like her first one with the late Francis Irie, Samuel could not wait to attend.

Speaking of marriage, he saw Grace drinking wine with her recently-wedded husband, Michel Bello. Samuel felt immensely grateful for Arisclan Bello's crucial help during the *War of the Osei Meadows* to the point that they too were raised in status, becoming Kingsclan Bello. Samuel was pleasantly surprised when Grace announced her desire to join their two families for good, and the Bello parents were thrilled that their son had asked for her hand in marriage. Jacqueline Bello was assumedly less thrilled, though no one knew for sure since the treacherous former friend of Grace's was being imprisoned in an underground dungeon.

An interesting blast from the past caught Samuel's eye. Deborah Lawal, Ezekiel's old love from his teenage years, was engaged in a passionate embrace with his older brother. She had rejoined their clan a year earlier after a brief stint as a dancer, *not* a pleasure-maiden, a distinction she thought was crucial to emphasise, to Samuel's amusement. She and Ezekiel enjoyed each other's company much more as of late. He would not be surprised if she and Ezekiel were thinking of settling down and starting a family, too.

Samuel wondered whether he should follow in his siblings' footsteps. But if he were to find love, it would have to wait. As the new leader of the Shared Council, he had a series of new policies he needed to implement to help develop his people and Civcaz as a whole.

The elder leader of the worshipping wanderers who had been the greatest help in restoring their clan, as far as Samuel was concerned, was awarded a place on said council and given the power to erect hundreds of new worship temples across the land.

Though their help was begrudging, Samuel rewarded the Irie family for their aid in battle by making them the new clan with the authority to host a large enough army to use in protecting the land from outside invaders. A role that was taken from the former Arisclan Rashid, who, for their allegiance to Osei in the meadow war, had been demoted to being a Commonsclan.

Samuel knew they would need these protections. He and the Saxe-Barbarians had parted after the War of the Osei Meadows on good terms, as he let Gideon Goldensight and his men keep all the gold and diamonds they pillaged from Osei's Hustan. But he knew they would not stay away for too long. The rogue barbarians were bound to become a problem in the future.

Samuel's most important policy was the one which he had wanted to install from the very beginning. The updated and revolutionised version of the training his father put him and his siblings through. The same training that prepared them for life very well, especially in their fight against the late Christian Osei.

The training system had been made into a youth development regimen that was implemented throughout most of Civcaz. Every day, he saw new budding warriors and polymaths. Ezekiel, having taken a break from his former job as a warmonger, acted as a key leader in this endeavour by teaching the children. Grace also offered a few lessons here and there alongside her brother, whilst Promise helped to finance their efforts.

Many people told Samuel that his father would have been exceptionally proud of him, his siblings, and all that they were doing.

But Samuel did not need to hear that. He already knew it. He could feel both his father's and mother's spirits in his heart. Kingsley and Faith Zhakkari's essences swirled together with all four virtues as they invigorated his soul.

With his new policies, Civcaz was finding it incredibly difficult to re-adjust, going through a long period of intense growing pains. Still, Samuel had faith in himself, in his siblings, and in the belief that all would be well.

THE AUTHOR

Jason Boje is a Nigerian-European author of science fiction, fantasy, crime, and young adult drama novels. He graduated with a Bachelor of Arts with Honours degree in Business Economics from Lancaster University in 2023, where he had developed his writing skills alongside his studies over the years. He has received numerous awards for several written works, including television screenplays and online novels.

CONNECT WITH JASON VIA:

Instagram: @jasonbojewriting

TikTok: @jasonbojewriting

YouTube: @jasonbtg